Also by Michael Bailey

Novels

Palindrome Hannah

Edited by Michael Bailey

Anthologies

Pellucid Lunacy

SCALES AND PETALS

STORIES & POEMS BY MICHAEL BAILEY

WWW.NETTIRW.COM

"The Seed" first appeared in *ART: MAG 27;* "Without Face" first
appeared in the magazine *Something Wicked, Issue 6* (South Africa);
"Defenestrate" first appeared in the anthology *In Bad Dreams: Vol. 1*
(Sweden); "The Box" first appeared online at *The Harrow;* "Feast of
Crows" first appeared online at *The Harrow;* "The Most Beautiful Place"
first appeared in the novel *Palindrome Hannah;* "Unstitched Love" first
appeared in the graphic anthology *Something Weird* (Australia), *Something
Weird Quarterly,* and later in *Something Wicked, Issue 11* (South Africa)

Published by Written Backwards
www.nettirw.com

ISBN: 978-1-7355981-5-4 / Hardback Edition
ISBN: 978-1-7327244-3-3 / Paperback Edition

SCALES AND PETALS

STORIES

BONUS CONTENT

POEMS

PLASTY

"What's that on your face?"

Thomas Parker took his change and examined the girl behind the counter. She wore a black Nine Inch Nails T-shirt with the words THE LINE BEGINS TO BLUR printed on the front. She had sun-deprived skin and red streaks running through her hair as if her scalp were bleeding. Mascara and shadow buried her eyes. Silver hoops pierced her eyebrows and the inner portions of her ears, and a silver stud poked through her nose like a small, metallic zit. There was a lot on her face.

He hadn't intended for the question to be so difficult. Thomas was referring to the dotted lines drawn onto her cheekbones, an upside-down triangle beneath each baggy eye. They resembled surgeons' marks.

She checked her reflection against the stainless steel espresso machine next to the register.

"What do you mean?"

Maybe they were tattoos.

"Never mind. Sorry."

She rotated one of the hoops in her ears, pinched the bottom of her nose. "Is there something on my face?"

Thomas signified the area over his own set of cheeks.

"Dotted lines … triangles?"

"What?"

"Here …" He leaned forward and traced the marks on her face with the tip of his finger.

She blushed and checked her reflection again and someone called out his drink order. Thomas grabbed his café mocha and snuck out before further embarrassment.

He collided with a woman chasing a child along the sidewalk. She caught the boy by his shoulder and spun him around. Her nose was covered with a patch of gauze and two horizontal strips of tape. Thomas's mocha spilled over the lid and onto his hand.

"I'm so sorry," she said, and then her nose started dripping onto the sidewalk. The gauze around her nostrils absorbed some of the blood.

"You're—"

"I know," she said. "Bobby's always taking off like that. Sometimes I wish I could put him on a leash."

"Your nose," said Thomas.

"What about it?"

"It's, uh … you have a nosebleed."

Her shirt striped red.

"What are you talking about?"

"Your nose is bleeding. You should see your doctor."

"What doctor? I don't know what you're talking about."

She grabbed her son and turned him away, leaving a bloody handprint on his shoulder.

"Come on, Bobby. We have an hour before cello."

The delusional woman wanted nothing to do with him.

She hailed a cab.

Thomas checked his pockets for Kleenex but came up empty, so he rushed into the coffee shop for some napkins to help stop the bleeding. Finding the container by the creams and sugars empty, he returned to the undead-looking girl at the counter.

The skin within the dotted lines on her face was missing; in place were two upside-down triangles of raw, skinless red, as if someone had cut the flesh and peeled it away.

"What?"

Thomas pointed to her jester eyes, backpedaling, and brushed against a woman standing behind him. One of her breasts tumbled within her blouse. It made an awful sound as it slipped out and plopped to the tiled floor. The silicone implant landed inches from his Skechers. He fetched it for her and held the hot, wet balloon in his hand before dropping it to the floor, realizing what it was.

"Watch where you're going."

Crimson blossomed at the flat area next to her other breast.

"Stop staring at my wife," said the man next to her. "What's your problem?"

Hesitating, Thomas retrieved the implant a second time. He held it out to them both with a shaky hand and said, "Your wife's breast—" as he pointed to her chest and inched the messy bag closer.

"Get your hand away from my wife."

The man slapped his hand away and pushed Thomas against the counter. A mug of coffee beans stabbed with pens spilled over and peppered the floor. The implant landed next to a poppy seed muffin purchased by the couple, covering part of it with clear, viscous matter. The single-breasted woman picked up the muffin and took a bite.

"Take this outside, you guys," said the barista behind the counter. The raw skin under her eyes dripped over the beans as she started to scoop them into the mug.

"I'm sorry," said Thomas. "I don't know what's happening to me. I don't know … I don't know what's happening, I—" but his words were cut short as he noticed the woman with the burnt face staring at him from across the lounge—a chemical peel. She bled from exposed pores as if her face had been ripped away. Everyone in and out of the coffee shop was some sort of failed plastic surgeon's nightmare. The woman outside with the nosebleed—a rhinoplasty; the woman with the single breast—some sort of mammoplasty; the young woman in line with the puffy lips …

"I—" His breath was all but gone as he said, "That guy by the couch." The guy by the couch had red gauze taped to his chin—a chin augmentation—which slid south and stuck to his neck. The bone was exposed, and for some reason Thomas remembered it was called a *mental protruberance*. The woman next to him stained a pair of white pants red at the crotch, perhaps from a labiaplasty gone horribly wrong.

The girl behind the counter with THE LINE BEGINS TO BLUR printed on her shirt, the young woman with the missing eye bags, she leaned over the counter and said, "Should I call an ambulance?" She plucked a cordless phone from the wall.

Thomas dizzied and crumpled to the floor. He formed into a fetal shape, grabbing a pain eating his stomach. When he pulled his hands away, they returned tacky and covered in a gelatinous, fatty substance. It was leaking from his stomach. He lifted his shirt to find a purple-brown bruise covering most of his abdomen, his bellybutton a loose flap of dead skin over a blackened hole.

Those in the coffee shop crowded around, their faces normal, their breasts natural, and their expressions horrified as they circled over him. The girl behind the counter with the piercings and the mascara and the streaks in her hair looked at Thomas Parker with the phone pressed to her ear. Her eyes were beautiful.

THE END OF TIME

or
THE SEED, PART ONE

You are more than a seed

Opening
You crack under pressure
Digging, reaching
Split symmetrically in protection
Loyal, faithful, unnecessary
Staying at your side as you reach blue

Surfacing
Fire burns through foamy cloud
Nourishing, aiding
You take in life, giving back what you can
Sprouting, rooting, budding
Your hands stretch out; body bursts a flower

Fertile
Striped strangers fly in new purpose
Burdens, treasures
You wait again for the red robin
Patient, serene, surrounded
The most magical thing in the world

You are more than a seed

HABIT

I used to bite my nails. Is the recorder on? Good. Yeah, so my nails … that's where the problem started. Mom would catch me in the habit. "Stop biting your nails," she'd tell me, "you'll never be able to stop." I used to gnaw on them, and at the hardened edges of skin around my nails. "You're only eating yourself," she'd say. "Is that what you want to do? You want to eat yourself? Like a cannibal?" I'd tell her no, but I'd do it anyway. There's probably a term or at least some kind of disease named for people who cannibalize on themselves. There's probably a self-help book for it. Some doctor wrote it. Some doctor who was beat as a child for biting his nails. I'd bite them so low sometimes my fingers would start to bleed. Then I'd suck at my fingertips till they went numb and start over again. I read somewhere once that if you drink blood your pee turns black. Is that true? Mom hated me asking her things like that. "Look at your cuticles," she'd say to change the subject. "You'll never be able to grow them long. You'll never be able to have them manicured. On your wedding day, all dressed in white, you'll have those horrid nails bleeding all over your dress." But that was before I lost my hands.

You could say my hands were misplaced, I guess, more than lost. They were misplaced between the rear tire of my Honda Civic and one of its fenders. A slip of the jack one weekend while replacing a flat and here we are. They weren't severed completely at the wrists; a few flaps of skin and tendon refused to let go. I remember Dad rushing out to help. He lifted the rear end of the car almost off the ground. I remember him reddening. I remember the vein poking out of his neck. I remember the expression on his face when I pulled two floppy appendages from the wheel well like a pair of wet gloves. Blood squirted from the ends of the skinny nubs attached to those gloves, but shock must have kept the pain away because I didn't scream until he grabbed me by the wrists and ran me into the garage. "Hold on, Lauren," he said, as if I could hold onto anything. "Just hold on."

He pulled me around his workbenches. My arms were cannons bellowing with every heartbeat. Blood was everywhere. I remember him slipping in it. We passed a group of storage containers when one of my hands detached and slapped onto the cement floor. We left it behind, but I half-expected it to start crawling after us. My other hand still dangled on as we came to a stop. Dad found what he was looking for: a box of coaxial cable. He let go of my nubs and pulled a few lengths of the black cable while I crumpled to the floor. I watched my life as it spilled from my wrists. I remember the hand and the splash of gore behind it, and the bloody stump where my arm abruptly ended. I remember trying to wiggle my fingers—on both hands—but they wouldn't move. But I felt them move somehow. I remember wondering how I could feel them as Dad knelt next to me with panic in his eyes as he knotted the cable around each of my wrists. He grabbed a screwdriver and threaded it underneath, and then he twisted clockwise, pinching the ends of my wrist—it cracked and squished and sealed shut and I nearly passed out from the pain—until it no longer bled.

He did the same to my other wrist until that hand also fell to the floor.

Dad drove me to the hospital. I don't remember much of the drive because I fell in and out of consciousness along the way, but I do remember Dad cussing me out for being so irresponsible … something about jacking the car on a hillside and fucking common-sense. Dad later told me he had forgotten to buckle me in, so when we screeched to a halt outside of Brenden Memorial, I smashed headfirst into the dashboard. I don't remember that, but he said it happened, so it must have happened. I woke up alone in a fuzzy white room on a morphine trip after some fucked up dreams.

I was out of it for at least five days. The accident happened on a Saturday afternoon and I remember the television mounted on the wall was playing a rerun of *The X-Files*, the episode written by Stephen King, and the show was in syndication Thursday nights. I remember trying to count the days on the fingers of my hand, but I could only count to one because I only had this nub, the ends of my radius and ulna bound together by a flap of skin and zigzags of black thread. The car had crushed the bones in that arm to mush, which is why my hand had fallen off so easily in the garage.

I asked Mom if I could keep the hands, or at least one—in a jar perhaps—but she refused. She said the hospital had to treat them as hazardous material and dispose of them properly. I can't imagine how they'd do such a thing, but she was probably right. Right?

"I brought your hands here in a cooler," she'd said to me. "All I could think about on my ride here was how bad your cuticles have gotten. The doctors even commented on it." That was a lie. The doctor's didn't give a piss about my cuticles.

"Even though I put them on ice, they said your wrists were too damaged and I don't think our insurance would've covered it anyway." I imagine a surgeon holding a needle in one hand, black thread in the other, sewing my hand onto my wrist like some kind of extension to a shirt sleeve. "Your father saved your life, you know," she had said. "If he hadn't thought of the tourniquets, you'd have bled to death." I remember raising one of my stumps. She had no idea I was flipping her off. Somewhere in the bio-hazardous waste—wherever the hospital stored it—there was a middle finger in the air.

She followed us to the hospital after finding my hands. I wonder how it felt to grab a hand without an arm attached to it, like some kind of rotten handshake. If she had pinched a finger, would I have felt it? What if I tried to grab her back? Would my fingernails still have tasted like my fingernails, or would it be like chewing on someone else's? She hated when I asked questions like that. It scared her that I sometimes felt phantom pains where my fingers used to be.

After six months of physical therapy, and a few rounds of psychotherapy like this little meeting, I returned to my old habits. I no longer had an inclination to bite my nails because, well, I didn't have any nails to bite, so I started slamming my arms against dresser drawers or the bathroom sink to remind myself I was still capable of feeling pain. Sometimes I still do it. Sometimes the ends of my wrists throb and I feel my pulse reaching out to ghost fingertips. If I could manage a blade, I'd probably cut myself. Not to kill myself, but to get that rush.

You know what I mean?

I'm a freak. Ever since my earliest memories, I wanted to be limbless. *Apotemnophilia*: the attraction of self-amputation. My last psychotherapist called it *Body Integrity Identity Disorder*, or

B.I.I.D. for short. He gave me a prescription for some crap that I never took and you'll probably do the same, I suspect. It won't work. I won't take anymore pills.

I never planned to lose *both* my hands. Just the one. I knew if I ruined a hand they'd have to chop it off. I read a few online articles about similar "accidents." I remember making sure Dad was in the garage to hear me scream. I remember parking my beat-up Honda Civic on a gravel incline and placing the jack under its frame before lifting the car. One bump and it would fall.

Mom calling me for dinner ruined everything. I was about to tell her I'd be a while when my hands met under the wheel well and my foot slid on the gravel and kicked the jack. If it weren't for Mom, today I'd be able to thumb a ride out of this shithole town. It's impossible to hitchhike with a nub. People want thumbs.

I can't blame Mom. She died almost a year after the incident. One night she was returning home from work and was struck head-on by a drunk driver. They said she died instantly. The driver of the other vehicle wasn't wearing his seatbelt. He was thrown through his windshield and through Mom's windshield and somehow landed in her seat with lacerations and a concussion but was otherwise fine. He's in prison now for vehicular manslaughter. He gets a couple years for killing her. Not quite a fair trade. When he gets out he'll hit the bottle again and kill someone else's mom.

It was a rough year with Dad. I don't know how he ever managed. Not only did he have the funeral, but also my routine doctor visits and physical therapy sessions. They wanted to try prosthetics, but we couldn't afford it. I still think of Mom whenever I get the sensations to bite my nails. Sometimes I chew my wrists to cope and I want to jump in front of a car. Sometimes they bleed and I hear her voice: "You're only eating yourself. Is that what you want to do? You want to eat yourself? Like a cannibal?" I picture myself in a wedding dress sometimes, bleeding all over it—a red wedding dress on a manikin with half-arms stretching straight out. I am seventeen and waiting for an armless prince to kiss me awake. Like that'll ever happen.

Instead, I don't have thumbs, I don't have fingers, and without Dad, I have no way to cut my food, tie my shoes, run baths, dress, or undress. I can't do anything normal on my own.

He pulled onto the side of the road one day and fell against the seat of the truck. We were on our way to buy some ice cream after one of my therapy sessions when he grabbed at his chest. He was going to get a cone for himself and a bowl for me. He was going to feed it to me because I couldn't hold a spoon. I couldn't move him; he was twice my weight, maybe more. I couldn't get him onto his back or out of the truck. I couldn't check his pulse. I remember placing one of my stumps under his neck, unable to feel anything. He was going to have chocolate and I was going to have chocolate and we were going to talk about Mom and visit her grave. We were going to discuss my problems. I remember my ghost fingers reaching for the door handle, but they wouldn't let me out to wave down help. I beat my nubs against the horn, hoping for someone to stop and lend a hand.

Are we done?

LOST

I need to watch things die
To know that I still live,
But from far away
So I stay sane.

You must kill me
To know that you love,
To know that you hate
To be without me.

I need to see myself bleed
To know that I can feel
Not just mechanical
As I sometimes seem.

You must cut me
To know that I am real
To know that I will cry
Underneath the blade.

I need to cease breathing
To know that I need air,
And drink the water
Until I drown.

You must suffocate me
To know that I don't breathe you,
To know that I don't need you
To fill my glass.

I need to break the mirror
To know that he's not real,
Only a stranger,
Without his soul.

You must hide me
To know that I won't find me,
To know that I won't try
To watch me die.

DEFENESTRATE

The first thing to fly out the window was the nineteen-inch television we had purchased when first moving in together, affixed bunny ears and all.

I watched as my wife hefted the thirty-pound tube toward the window, its heaviness revealed by her stressing muscles and shaky legs. The top rested against her cheeks and smashed the curves of her face into awkward angles. She stopped at the sill. I rose from my chair and helped her by unlatching the lock. Old painted wood scraped across old painted wood as the framed, single-pane glass lifted. She catapulted the television from her body.

We lived on the fourth floor of an apartment complex, a brick getup downtown with weathered awnings that no longer held original color. We often leaned out to smell the rusty air between our dilapidated building and the next, sometimes wedging a cigarette between our fingers. The smoke was refreshing, different anyway than the smog and the rotting who-knows-what in the dumpsters below. We'd sit on the painted two-by-six that acted as what the advertisement for the place had called "a balcony view." This is where the television paused in flight.

The Mitsubishi's wingless migration to the sidewalk ended short as its featherless tail, the power cord, caught between the window and the windowsill. The television swung and smacked against brick and mortar. Cassie shrugged with frustration, her fists clenched with whitened knuckles. She grunted, hunting for further possessions with similar yearnings to fly. I had a few objects in mind she could throw out—our wedding rings, for starters.

Our marriage was a con from the start—she a Catholic, me an atheist. Her parents hated my parents; they never spoke to one another. The same went for Cassie and me through our long and pathetic marriage.

We were doomed to failure the moment we gave our vows. Vows could be thrown out as well: to have and to hold; she could hold on to *them* as *they* flew out the window. How we ever managed to stay together for ten years is beyond my comprehension. This fight wasn't the first, either. It was a small battle in the great epic war saga of our relationship.

A collection of Edgar Allan Poe missed knocking my block off by a few pages. I could almost feel the old leather binding graze my brow. It made the miniscule hairs on the nape of my neck stand on end as the compilation flew in gracious slow-motion. Pages flapped at cold air. The word "raven" crossed my vision. If it had happened any slower, I could have finished the brilliant poem: "*And the satin sad uncertain rustling of each purple curtain as things I never thought important pass by my face forever more.*" Right then I recalled one of his short stories in which the main character buries another man alive behind brickwork. It made me wonder how difficult (or easy, for that matter) it might be to hide Cassie—my beloved wife Cassie—somewhere in the brickwork of the apartment building we called home. "*Screaming in agony, forever more.*"

As time caught up with me, more books took flight. I watched *The Great Gatsby* flutter by in an unsteady arc. A bird with one wing could fly more amiably. A flock of *Robinson Crusoe*, *Treasure Island*, and *The Swiss Family Robinson* soared through the air. They struggled with new offered buoyancies, and then their characters found new cement shores on the cracked sidewalk below.

Trying to reason with Cassie was out of the equation. It was 'everything must go' at the Williams Manor. Getting in the way would stir the pot and lead to unfathomable injuries.

I kicked the power cord lodged in the windowsill and it whipped through the air. The television fell … fell … fell (one more floor to go) … fell, and crash! It made an awful sound as the monstrous vacuum in the cathode ray tube exploded. I couldn't watch, but imagined shards of glass raining over my discarded possessions like after-party glitter on New Year's Day.

"Don't forget my records," I told her, but she had already gathered a stack and was removing their protective cardboard sheaths. She broke a few of the vinyl discs over her knee before losing interest. I handed her an empty shipping box. She filled it and dropped it out the window. Soon to follow were movies, video games, board games and mixed collectibles from over the years.

I had realized by this point that the sooner this event ended, the sooner I could get on with my life. I grabbed an armful of clothing from the oak dresser in our bedroom and tossed them out.

On one of my trips to and from the bedroom, I was stopped dead in my tracks by a framed photograph propped on the headboard of the bed we had slept in (and only slept in) for the duration of our marriage.

We had hiked through the wild terrain of Yosemite—roughly ten miles—for most of the morning and into the late afternoon, until we came across what we later learned was the Nevada Falls. A beautiful spectacle: water churning over pepper-speckled granite, foliage surviving through cracks in the mammoth boulders, the millions upon millions of gallons of water, the wildlife in the sky, squirrels crawling along the rocks. It was a scene of pure beauty as we crossed over the water-fall's drainage. The long bridge took us over water a few inches deep in places, maybe a foot or two in others. The recent snow covered the earth around us in a thin blanket. We had crossed paths with two other hikers, one of which snapped the picture. We faced the camera with the falls dropping behind us, stocking caps pulled over our ears, smiles on our faces.

We were in love. Of course, back then my belongings weren't getting thrown out the window, so loving her was a little easier to manage. You often hear the term 'falling out of love' with couples that experience difficulties and later find themselves separated. I don't believe we ever "fell." Maybe there was never a place set for us from which we could fall. Perhaps our place never sat high enough—a molehill in comparison to the mountain peaks good relationships can become. The photograph captured the last time Cassie and I ever smiled as a pair.

I flipped over the frame and unlatched the black, felt-covered cardstock and removed the frozen memory. The captured still held so much within its four-by-six stature. It would take a novelist to unravel the words necessary to describe our happiness and our love at that precise moment in time. After studying our last sparkle—our last flame—for what seemed hours, the picture made its way to my shirt pocket for me to take as a keepsake.

The cloud of noise from the living room dissipated. Eeriness grazed my spinal cord and poked each vertebra with needles. Gooseflesh swam beneath my skin as I realized fiery eyes were burning holes into my back. I felt them attach like magnets to my own as I spun around.

It was Cassie, but something was different about her. She no longer possessed the demon I had grown to love to hate to despise yet admired yet loathed and felt I had to love or to kill or to strangle to death with the vise of my grip so that we again could ... what, *love?* No, this was not that woman; this was my dear Cassie. *The* Cassie who had held my hand through school and had kissed my lips ever so gently every time one of us spotted a green car. That was our color. It was a game we invented so our lips could play more often than they probably should have. Green M & Ms counted as well. They make you horny, it is rumored. They did for us anyway, back then.

Cassie stood before me holding a green toy car. I had no idea the make or model and couldn't have cared less; it was her gaze that captured me, the same gaze that had captured me ten years ago when we first met. She stepped closer and said she loved me. She said she would always love me. Tears traced her cheeks, but they were sorrowful and filled with love. We smiled childish smiles and embraced. Our mouths locked onto each other. I could feel the air being sucked from my face. I pulled back, but not for much more than a breath, before she bit my bottom lip (on accident?) and reaffixed her lips to mine.

She groped my back with razor nails and worked wonders with her snake tongue. Memories of previous encounters between us flushed warm blood to my head and confusion to my mind. *How long had it been? What had come between us? Is this even right?* She pressed her body against mine and we magically fit together as one. This time *she* had to gasp for breath. She bit my ear lobe and whispered how she loved me so. We kissed each other's necks and our bodies melted. Everything felt wonderful felt right felt wrong. At the brisk sound of glass breaking, I again was alone.

I found that Cassie wasn't with me in the bathroom, but still in the living room tossing possessions of mine out the window. The magical encounter between us never occurred; my subconscious apparently had a sense of humor. I had blood on my hands—not much, but enough to jumpstart my heart. The glass from the picture frame was now a symmetric pair of sine waves. A greenish translucent curve split the middle and had cut into my palm, where a thin line of red welled. It didn't hurt, but it bled profusely. I dropped the frame and pulled apart the now-sectioned flat part of my hand known to palm readers as 'the love line.' The irony in this was inherently evil.

I then gathered what few of my belongings I cherished and stashed them away so they wouldn't take flight.

I patched my hand with a bandage after scrounging for one under the sink. In the distance I could hear Cassie yelling who-knows-what. It was easily ignorable background noise, though my name was mixed in there on occasion.

The sound of something made of either porcelain or china crashed at my feet on the white bathroom tile. I was leaning on the counter with both hands. I tilted my head to catch her reflection with mine in the mirror. The cut on my hand was not quite subdued, the pain still there. Cassie's eyes burned into mine as it had in the daydream. Sweat developed at her brow. Tiny droplets made their way downward to meet whatever she had thrown at my feet. Her cheeks flushed with rage. It was a rage I had accommodated over the years and passed off as unbalanced hormones or mood swings. Now, in this false image, this twisted reflection of hers in the mirror, I could tell it was much more than that; it was a need for control, a need for power—it didn't matter over what, but it was with me.

"Why don't you just pack your bags and leave, Kyle?" It was more of a demand than a question and she made my name sound like a swear word. Her body heaved in and out with each heavy breath. *You know you can't,* her eyes read. *You know you can't,* Kyle, *because you still love me,* Kyle.

"I still think I do," I mumbled.

Another crash filled the bathroom as she smashed a second item. This time a broken shard met my ankle and I couldn't help but see what she was bombarding me with: the head of a raven. Its beady red eyes dug a hole into my chest. Pieces of the black bookend were scattered around. Half of a second head lay by the toilet, part of the bookend twin.

Cassie had crossed a line this time. I treasured nothing more than my raven bookends. They were an anniversary present several years ago—the year of the Yosemite trip. She found them at an antique shop. They were old, a hundred and twenty years at least, and carved from rock that resembled obsidian, but duller. The eyes were possibly rubies. Cassie had given me the set with much thought and with much intended love. I had cherished the gift the way I would have cherished children if we ever managed any. Now they were nothing more than broken memories. Nevermore.

Imagination seized my mind. I envisioned leaning down to retrieve the heaviest of the remaining fragments, and driving it into her skull. Her head would break apart. Her likewise red eyes would stare at me from the floor. Her figure would lay limp. I would then lift her body, lug it to the windowsill, and throw it onto the pile with the rest of my crap. The same body I had once made love to, and had loved to make love to—a heap adding to the pile like yesterday's garbage.

A smile emerged on my reflected face.

I snatched the head of a raven, twirling it within my hand (wouldn't take much to smash it into her face, now would it?). My pulse rose from a steady tempo to an insane beat. After a slight hesitation, I chucked it at the mirror. The mirror cracked in several places but not a single shard fell to the floor; three main sections held what remained of the mirror in place on the wall. Cassie's face was broken into three separate reflections. The first showed a crooked mouth, the second her hot-tempered cheeks, and the third a pair of horrorstricken, disbelieving eyes.

We stood in silence long enough for our pulses to return to semi-normalcy, and long enough for the blood cells behind our skin to disperse and lighten our bodies from angry scarlet to exhausted pale. We shed tears and cried for each other in an interlude void of words.

And then, as the distant sound of sirens filled our ears, the fighting started all over again.

"This is Officer Milton. Please open up. I don't want to have to kick in this door." A couple pounds from her nightstick and then, "I've had a very long day. Please open—"

I opened the door and she entered. One of her hands held a nightstick, the other rested on the latch to her 9mm Glock. She was ready to draw; most likely in the time it would take me to blink. Officer Milton apparently had no idea what to expect.

"Sorry if we've been causing a disturbance," I said. "My wife and I were arguing and things got a little out of hand."

As if to prove I wasn't beating the life out of her, Cassie appeared from the hallway. "Is everything all right, officer?"

The officer considered the mess in the apartment. Her face transformed into a jumbled expression of relief, humor and condolence. She attached the nightstick to her belt and set her hands at ease. She started to smile, but then she stopped herself, authority filling its place. She grabbed a notepad from her jacket pocket.

"You two were arguing?"

"We're sorry about the noise?" Cassie said.

"And you are …?"

"Cassie Williams. And this is Kyle, my husband." It took a lot for her to admit this. She pointed my way. Although my name still sounded cursed, I couldn't help but feel … *pride?*

The officer jotted our names, said, "Just arguing, huh?"

Cassie and I nodded.

"Are you aware," she started, but hesitated, "that there is a pile of miscellaneous objects pointing to your apartment from below? Books, clothes …"

We both nodded.

Officer Milton scribed more onto her miniature notepad and evaluated the mess. Tables were upturned, desk drawers emptied out, broken glass and tidbits of paper spread everywhere.

"What a mess."

She made her way around the room, continuously writing. She stopped at the window, peeked out and shook her head. "Which one of you tossed out the television? I bet that was a load of fun."

Cassie raised her hand.

"Actually," I interjected, and as well took the glory, if you could name it that, "she threw it out, yes. But the power cord jammed in the windowsill. I kicked the cord loose. So it was really my doing."

Was it love that made me say it? Was it that same love we had shared so long ago that I recognized in the details of her face? Was there still love in that cold, black heart of hers?

"I see," the officer said. "Can you come here, sir?"

I joined her at the window. It was a pyramidal tower, more than anything you could label as a pile. There were boxes and compact discs and collectibles and shirts, shoes, socks, hats, pants, boxers, thousands (it seemed) sheets of paper, our photo albums, and the aforementioned nineteen-inch Mitsubishi television—the same television I was never able to let go of until today, when I had let it go out the window. Cassie had begged and begged over the years to replace it, but I could never let it go.

"Man, the TV is thrashed," I said and grinned.

And then she said the words I will never forget for as long as I live; one single sentence—a question really—that would change my life forever: "It's thrashed, yeah ... but do you see the arms and legs coming out from under it?"

MON AUTUMN

Little pieces from me fall,
Jagged-jigsaw bits of memory.
I try pounding them back in place,
But they no longer fit;
The necks just bend.

And so they fall / no longer fit.

Little pieces from me fall,
Wadded-sticky bits of mind.
I try gluing them back together,
But they no longer stick;
They just fall apart.

And so they fall / no longer stick.

Little pieces from me fall,
Fast-forgotten bits of past.
I try, I try, I try to remember,
But they no longer stay;
They just go away.

And so they fall / no longer stay.

Little pieces,
These little pieces from me,
These things,
They fall.
I try,
These things,
But, like weathered leaves,
They crumble at my feet.
I step on my mind,
A labyrinth mind,
My mind,
All but ash.
Within my fingertips
Lies
My past.
I try,
These things,
Forcing them back inside,
But they no longer live.
They just get smashed.

And so they fall / no longer live.

WILTED FLOWERS

In the fall of 1987, things began to disappear from the Mallory home. Not only were the leaves in the plentiful oaks abandoning their homes to dry up and fall to the ground, or the sun vanishing earlier and earlier each night behind the valley's shadowy mountain range, and not even the school children removing themselves from backyards to return to their classrooms, but the disappearance of solid objects in general, such as Allison Mallory's socks and her brother Peter's autographed Wade Boggs rookie card. Everything that went into the chest never came out once the lid closed.

It was Peter who found it. After their grandmother had passed away that summer, there was much to go through. Most of her boxed belongings were donated to Hennisen's, the local thrift shop on Sudbury Lane. Some of it, heirlooms, keepsakes, and various articles of jewelry, were divided amongst their aunts, uncles and, of course, Allison and Peter's parents. Everything else smelled of mildew, mold, or decay, and was eventually stored in the basement until it was sorted through or thrown out. In the single light bulb illuminated basement, underneath a box of rat-chewed books and letters, waited the chest.

"Whoa," said Peter, signifying both his discovery, as well as the stench. He pushed off the box of papers, spilling its contents to the ground. His camouflage T-shirt instantly gained a new dusty gray to its many colors. He had to move a few dust-filled scraps of old linen and brown-cloudy jars of expired canned fruits that had been in the basement for probably years. The chest groaned as Peter started to pull it free from the junk around it. Allison joined him in the basement as he was about to prop open the lid.

"What's that?" she asked.

Allison had turned fourteen the week before. If her brother were the older of the siblings, a snide comment might have followed, but he was mesmerized by his discovery and a full three years younger.

He pulled at the chest again, scraping lines into the foundation, and jimmied it into the open. It was nearly double his size. He could easily hide from his sister inside.

The chest was at least a century or two old, well-crafted and weathered. It was heavy, mostly metal, and leavened with straps of leather around its surface, all of which appeared an oily dark brown, almost blackened in places, as if it had survived a fire at one point in its travels. There were handles on each side, one of them broken. A rusted metal latch kept the chest sealed, but there wasn't a lock to keep anyone out of it. Carved into the lid were words neither Allison nor Peter recognized: GEWELKT SCHNITTBLUMEN

"Anything could be in there," said Allison, her eyes wide. She pulled her dirty-blonde hair into a ponytail.

"Whatever's in here, it's mine," said Peter. "I found the chest."

"I'm sure Mom would disagree. Whatever's in there would be Mom's, or Aunt Lisa's, or Uncle James's. They'd have to split it evenly. But who cares, open it. I want to see what's in there."

Apparently, so did Peter. He struggled a bit with the latch, but managed to figure it out. It took both hands to lift and finally push open the top half of the chest. The mammoth lid creaked on its un-oiled hinges and startled them both as it came crashing against the other side. The right-most hinge snapped because of the weight.

At first, Peter thought the chest was empty. All he could see in the poor basement lighting was black, a treasure of nothing. Peter peered inside, squinting. Allison leaned in closer.

"It's empty," she said. "Maybe Grandma used to keep stuff in there, like photo albums or something."

Peter reached inside, felt around for a while, and returned with a handful of dead flowers bound together with a strip of twine.

"Here," he said, "these are for you. You get the treasure."

He searched the crevices inside, but found nothing more than shriveled leaves and wilted petals.

"Thanks." Allison rolled her eyes.

"Think Mom will let me keep the chest?" asked Peter.

"Why do you want it?"

"I don't know. Maybe to keep stuff in it."

"I wouldn't want to put anything in there. It smells like old books. The entire basement smells like a library. She'll probably let you have it, though. Unless she wants it for some reason."

Peter attempted to lift the chest by the unbroken handle. It rose an inch from the ground before breaking.

"Can you help me bring it upstairs?" Peter pushed it a few inches at a time. Scratch marks stayed behind on the floor, the chest indeed too heavy for him to carry alone.

"If you want it, you can find a way to get it upstairs."

"Fine. I will."

With much effort, Peter continued pushing and pulling at

the enormous chest. He stopped for a moment at the stairs and lifted one end onto the first step.

Allison stepped around her brother and the chest, heading out with her dried bouquet of flowers. "I'm gonna put these in water," she joked.

For the next half-hour, Peter worked the old chest up the basement stairs, pushing mostly from behind. Twice the chest, nearly at the top of the stairwell, loosened from his hold and slid to the bottom. He smashed a few of his fingers and almost had the chest on top of him at one point. But, eventually, he made it to the top, across the kitchen floor with a few nasty scrapes, through the dining room, the hallway, and finally to the middle of his bedroom. Grooves dug into the carpet, outlining his path.

Peter's room was across from Allison's. She stepped in to see what he was doing after a while, holding the dried flowers in a vase.

"So, what are you going to put in there?"

Peter wiped his sweaty brow. His hair was a mess, pressed flat with perspiration in places. He took a deep breath, contemplating.

"I don't know."

"That's *if* Mom lets you keep it. It smells funny."

"You smell funny."

Peter scouted the bedroom for something to put in the chest. Baseball posters covered the walls. Mountains of laundry were piled around his bed. And then his eyes connected to one of his dressers. The junk drawer was at the top, in which he kept his not-so-secret stash of allowance money, his favorite toys, cassette tapes and, of course, his most valuable of baseball cards. The drawer contained miscellaneous LEGO pieces, puzzle ends, candy, some old coins, fireworks, but it was his collection of cards Peter was drawn to first add to the chest. The chest would be his new junk drawer.

He pushed it farther into this room and to the gap between his bed and the wall. Again, Peter lifted the lid and peered inside. He removed the few remaining flower petals and threw them to a carpet in desperate need of vacuuming. Using a dirty shirt— also from the floor—he wiped the inside of the chest.

Allison stood at his bedroom door.

"You can put *these* in there," she said, launching a balled pair of her own socks to the old trunk. The lid slammed shut and made them both jump.

"Quit it," he said, going to the chest.

Upon lifting the lid once more, Peter was surprised the socks hadn't landed inside.

"Did they bounce off?"

"They're not *in* the trunk," he said, "or anywhere around it." He pillaged the dirty clothes and garbage on the floor.

"Maybe if you cleaned your room once a year—"

"They're right here," he said, holding a pair.

"My socks aren't brown and holey."

"Your face is brown and holey," he said, still rummaging, his arm reaching deep under the bed.

"That doesn't make sense. *You don't make sense*," she mocked. "Anyway, I want them back if you ever find them. I'll be in my room. My *clean* room."

As soon as Allison left, Peter stopped searching for her socks. He couldn't care less about her socks or where they'd disappeared. All he cared about was filling the chest so Mom would be less inclined to not let him keep it. He knew how she worked.

The first thing to go in was Wade Boggs. His rookie card. Peter could tell because only the first year of stats were printed on the back. He could still smell the bubble gum. When he bought the Topps pack years ago, he found the Boggs card inside, a hard stick of pink gum stuck against it. He'd always chewed the gum, no matter how bad the taste. It was all part of growing up. Peter never enjoyed watching baseball on television, but he loved playing the sport and, for some reason, loved collecting baseball cards more.

Wade Boggs was his favorite. Peter knew the card would be valuable someday; he kept it in a plastic sleeve to keep the corners from bending. His dad told stories of how they'd all be rich today if their grandmother hadn't thrown out his own collection of baseball cards. "I collected all the good ones, too," he'd say, "like Mantle, Williams, Aaron and Ruth." Everyone's father seemed to have a similar story.

The single card made the trunk seem enormous. Wade looked lonely in there, so Peter added Nolan Ryan, Mike Schmitt, and the entire Boston Red Sox lineup, banded together like playing cards.

He was about to add Mariners when Allison returned.

"Mom says dinner's ready."

Without a word, Peter abandoned the open chest and followed his sister to the kitchen table.

The wondrous smell of roast beef filled the kitchen, slow roasted with potatoes and carrots in the oven. Garlic-buttered sourdough bread baked on the top rack, just browning on their edges as Anna Mallory removed the tray and set it onto a pair of hotplates waiting on the table. Next to it was the roast.

"Where's Dad?" asked Allison.

"He's working late."

Peter reached for toast. "Dad always works late."

"That's because your father wants there to be food on the table for all of us." Anna pulled portions of roast onto all three plates and spooned out vegetables. "He should be home soon."

"Shouldn't we wait?" asked Allison.

"No. He called earlier and said not to wait. I'll make Paul a plate and put it in the fridge." The kitchen clock was taunting. She wiped away developing tears and sat to eat.

"What's wrong?" asked Allison.

"Nothing's wrong. It's the garlic. What did you kids do this afternoon? I heard you in the basement making all sorts of noise."

"We found a chest," said Peter, his mouth full of food. He crammed more in with his fork, trying to finish his dinner early.

"A chest?"

"And flowers," added Allison. "A bouquet of dead flowers."

"Your grandmother's chest? I haven't seen that in years. You found it in the basement?"

"Yeah. Peter's got it in his room."

"Can I keep it, Mom," he said, "to put *my* stuff in?" Peter's plate was nearly clean. He chugged his glass of milk.

"He didn't ask if he could have it," informed Allison.

"Well, you didn't ask if you could have the flowers.".

Anna tried making sense of it all.

"They were in the chest," said Allison.

Anna changed her focus to her plate. "A long time ago, long before you kids were born, my mother kept an old weathered chest at the foot of her bed. She said it was off limits, and that we were never to open it, or to look inside."

"Did you ever look inside?" asked Peter.

"Only once." Anna worked her fork around her plate, moving the food around, not interested in eating.

"She told your aunt and me it was a place to put things you wanted to forget. A place to put things you never wanted to see again. Maybe it's not hers. What does it look like?"

Peter chimed in: "It's old and dusty, smells like books, and has some strange words on the front."

"It's German," said Anna. "*Gewelkt schnittblumen* ... I used to give your grandmother things to put in the chest. One time Lisa and I got into a fight. We were about your age. Out of spite I snuck into her room and took her favorite doll. I always hated her for having it, mostly because I wanted it for myself. It was ceramic and I dropped it while playing with it outside."

"Did it break?" asked Peter.

"The head broke. In two. Lisa was at a friend's, and I knew she'd be home soon, so I buried it behind the house. I was little and didn't know what else to do."

"Did she ever notice it missing?" asked Allison.

"She noticed the moment she stepped into her room. She came barging into mine, accusing me of taking it. I lied to her face and told her I'd never take it. We got into a bigger argument and she said if I didn't give it back by morning she'd kill me. Your aunt would never kill me, but I was gullible at that age and actually believed her. But still, I lied and said I didn't take it.

"For the next few hours I cried into my pillow, unsure what to do. Your grandmother must have heard me crying, because she came in and sat next to me on the bed. I was shaking, bawling. I admitted everything. How we got into a fight. How I took her doll, accidentally broke it and buried it in the backyard. How Lisa would kill me in the morning.

"Before dinner that night, she went with me to unbury it. I held the doll in my hands. The head was broken in two, her dress caked in mud. She told me she'd put it in the chest. The place to put things you never wanted to see again.

"She took the doll, put it in the chest, and then drove me to the store to buy your aunt a new doll. She told me to give it to Lisa in the morning, to apologize and tell her the truth, by admitting I took the doll."

"Did she ever find out?" asked Allison.

"Not then. She took the doll and never said a word." Anna smiled. "I told her after we were both moved out of the house."

"What was inside the chest?" asked Peter. "The one time you looked inside."

"I was eighteen when I finally opened it. Until that time, Lisa and I—I'm sure—had given her many things to put in there during the course of our childhood. Many ugly memories we wanted to forget at the time."

"Was it full?" asked Peter.

"No, but it wasn't empty, either. The day I looked in the chest was the same day your grandfather died. He and your grandmother had gotten into a nasty fight the night before. He stayed in a motel to give her space. All night I listened to her cry.

"The next morning, your grandfather placed a bouquet of roses on the kitchen counter, with a note saying how sorry he was for everything. The flowers were his apology; his way of saying he still loved her.

"Later that morning, we got a knock on the door. A police officer told us your grandfather had pulled over to the side of the road and had passed away."

Anna wiped tears from her face.

"I remember I was eating a fried egg sandwich. I remember

crying with food in my mouth. That same day, I looked in the chest to remember all the things I had earlier wanted to forget. The chest was empty, except for the wilted flowers from your grandfather."

"Where's my Boggs card, Allison?"

"Your what?"

"My autographed Wade Boggs rookie card," said Peter, "and all my other cards. You took 'em from my chest."

"You mean *Grandma's* chest."

"No, *my* chest. Now give them back!"

"I didn't take your cards. I don't even like baseball."

"Fine. I'll take *these* until you give them back."

Peter grabbed the dead flowers from the vase on her dresser. A few petals broke free and fell around its base.

Before Allison could react, he was out the door.

"Those are mine!" She followed him to his room. "Mom said I could have those … I didn't take your stupid cards!"

Peter slammed the lid the moment Allison walked into the room. A plume of dust escaped the cracks.

"Give them back."

Peter sat on top of the chest.

"You give back my cards. You're jealous Mom let me keep the chest and all you got were some dead roses."

"They're sentimental."

"My cards are sentimental."

"You don't even know what that means. Now *move!*"

Allison nearly pushed him off.

Peter grabbed onto the sides.

"Move!"

They wrestled, Peter nearly as tall as his sister while atop the chest. They were interrupted by their mother.

"What's all the commotion about?" she asked, separating them. "You should be getting ready for bed."

"Peter stole Grandma's flowers from my dresser."

"That's because she took my cards."

"What cards?" she asked.

"All my *good* cards."

"I did not!"

"Yes you did. I put them in my chest and you took 'em cause all you got were those stupid flowers!"

"That's enough. Both of you."

"But—" they both began.

"Enough! Peter, where are the flowers?"

Peter hopped off the chest and creaked it open.

She grabbed the bundle and handed them to Allison.

"These are very fragile, so take good care of them. They meant a lot to your grandmother and mean a lot to me."

"But, Mom—" Peter was interrupted by the superpower of his mother's index finger and piercing glare.

"Allison, where are your brother's cards?"

Allison's eyes met the carpet. She shrugged.

"Where are your brother's cards? Look at me," she said, lifting Allison's chin so that their eyes met.

"I don't know," Allison whined.

"We'll sort this out in the morning. Both of you brush your teeth and get to bed. It's late."

At a quarter to midnight, Paul's truck pulled into the driveway, that familiar sound of gravel crunching under tires. The engine settled. The driver door opened, closed. Anna listened for his footsteps. Paul, working late again. He had worked late three days a week now, it seemed. Each night a little later than the next. He called Anna each time, told her not to wait for dinner, sometimes not to wait for bed. Stuck at the office, he'd say. Come to find out, *The Office* was the name of a bar downtown off Jasper Road.

She listened as Paul unlocked the front door to the house. He tossed his keys onto the end table. Anna couldn't help but place visualizations with each sound: the fridge, the microwave heating his dinner, dirty dishes rattling in the sink, the wisp of a beer opening, Paul changing out of his clothes and sliding into bed. He was asleep in minutes. He reeked of booze and an unfamiliar perfume that had started becoming all-too-familiar as of late.

Anna stared out the window, to the moon, tears welling around her eyes. She thought of Allison and Peter, feuding over the littlest of things, how she had once believed her sister Lisa would actually have killed her over something as petty as a doll, Mom always settling everything, Mom having that secret place to put things you'd rather forget, the chest, the dirty doll with the broken face, the wilted flowers …

"Your socks!" said Peter. "They disappeared!"

Allison rubbed her eyes. Her alarm clock said it was way too early for a Saturday morning. The sun had yet to rise.

Peter dragged her by an arm to his room.

"The socks," he said. "I thought they might have rolled under the bed, but they're gone. They're with my cards now."

Allison gave Peter a charlie horse and yawned.

"What was *that* for?"

"For lying."

"No, honest. Watch!"

Peter searched frantically around his room for something he no longer wanted, or needed, something not *his* perhaps. His eyes widened as he spotted the wadded camouflage shirt near the foot of his bed from the previous day.

"This is stupid, Peter. Your cards are not—"

"Just watch."

He then headed to the old chest, lifted the lid and dropped the shirt, grinning.

"Wow … impressive. Can I go back to bed now?"

"Close the lid," said Peter.

"This is stu—"

"Just do it."

Allison marched hesitantly to the chest and closed it.

"Now open it."

"I just closed it."

Allison rolled her eyes and lifted the lid. She peered inside, then to her brother, and then to the empty chest.

"How'd you do that?"

Allison reached around inside, finding dust with her fingertips. She looked around the chest. Maybe her brother had played a trick, dropping it behind, or around. *But I watched him drop it in.*

"How'd you do that?"

"I didn't do anything. It's the chest. Like Mom said: it's a place to put things you wanna forget."

"And you wanted to forget your camo shirt?" She continued to hunt the room for his missing T-shirt.

"Well, no, not exactly. But it was dirty, so I guess so."

"Let's try to forget something else," she said.

"Like what?"

"How about this?" She grabbed a half transformed Optimus Prime from his bed. Apparently, before this great discovery, Peter had started a war on his comforter between his collection of Autobot and Decepticon Transformers. Allison gingerly tossed the red, metal toy into the chest.

"No, wait!" Peter held out his hand. "Well … okay. Go for it." Again he smiled. It seemed he could use some new toys after all.

Allison peered inside. "It's still there."

"You have to close the lid."

She closed it. "How long do we wait?"

"I dunno," said Peter, "a millisecond."

Allison opened the lid and poor Optimus Prime was no more.

"Whoa!"

"Pretty cool, huh?" Peter scrunched his eyes, probably regretting losing his lost toy, once one of his favorites. "But I'm not sure where they go. They just disappear."

"So Mom's story is true," she said. "Grandma used to get rid of all those things Mom and Aunt Lisa wanted to forget. I wonder where *she* got it?"

"I don't know, some place in Germany, but it looks really old. I bet there's some place in the world where all this stuff ends up. There's probably a huge pile somewhere. And now it has Optimus on top, and my camo shirt, your dirty socks, Boggs, and my other cards. And *loads* of other cool stuff.

"Maybe everything that goes inside disappears forever, another dimension or another time. Remember those *Dark Tower* books where there were doors that led to other places?

"I bet it goes somewhere. And wherever it goes, there's a

big mound of treasure. Maybe this was once a pirate chest and some captain with a parrot on his shoulder and an eye patch used it to hide his loot."

Allison shrugged. "Maybe."

"Let's try some other stuff," said Peter.

"Like what?"

"Let's try something weird."

"Something weird?"

"Yeah," said Peter. "I'll be back."

Peter ran out of the bedroom. In seconds he returned with a glass of tap water. He was quite the experimentalist.

"Mom will ground you if you lose one of her glasses."

Peter thought about it, and instead of placing the filled glass inside the chest, he dumped the water inside. He quickly closed the lid, opened it, and the chest was dry.

They both smiled.

"This is *so* strange," said Allison. "Wait … when we first found the chest, there were the dead flowers inside. Grandma put those in, but *they* didn't disappear. And earlier you put 'em back in and closed the lid and they didn't disappear then, either … Let's try something else."

Peter thought a moment and went to his junk drawer where he had once kept his collection of baseball cards. He pulled out a belt of cheap firecrackers from last summer's trip across the states. The Mallory family had stopped at one of those firework stands in Wyoming, where nearly all types of explosives were legal. They had stopped there and bought some fun to help celebrate the July 4th holiday and his mother had let him keep what they hadn't used for the following summer. Peter pulled out a lighter.

"Where'd you get a cigarette lighter?"

"From a friend at school," he said, as if reciting something as mundane as a phone number.

Allison watched her brother with anticipation.

Without a second thought, Peter lit the entire string of fireworks and tossed them into the chest. He closed the lid as both he and Allison waited for the machinegun fire.

After some silence, Allison raised the lid. The firecrackers were gone. Not even the smells of sulfur or burnt wick remained.

"Allison, Peter!"

They both jumped.

"Breakfast!"

"Mom can't find out about this," said Allison. "At least not yet."

"You don't think she already knows about the chest?"

"No."

"Why not?"

"Because," said Allison, "she let you keep it."

Prior to breakfast, Anna ran a few loads of laundry. She was used to reversing pockets for loose change, mostly to remove toys and candy wrappers and such from Peter's pants, so the act of reversing the pockets of all to-be-washed—or warshed, as her own mother would say—clothing came as second nature. Sometimes she'd find a five or a twenty, or the occasional entirely forgotten wallet. Such was the case with the pants Paul had worn the night prior while "working late." He'd left this morning without his wallet …

She thought of snooping inside. Who was she to nose her way into her husband's affairs? *Maybe it* was *an affair. Maybe inside*

I'll find proof. Anna placed it close to her face and smelled the leather. *What am I hoping to smell? The stench of money? A hint of that strange perfume? A reason Paul had to go in this morning for work—a Saturday of all days—when never in fourteen years of marriage had he ever worked weekends?* She peeked inside.

The billfold contained thirteen dollars: two fives, three ones. A few receipts were folded behind the bills, nothing new. One was for Temple Grounds Coffee down the street, totaling $3.50, or one drink; the other was for The Colonel. Paul had picked up a bucket of chicken a few evenings ago for dinner. It was his night to cook, in other words, and a night he didn't have to "work late." In their proper places, Anna found the gas card, Paul's ATM Check Card, some mangled business cards and

(no, anything but)

hidden behind those mangled business cards

(a wad of paper a Post It a reminder another stupid receipt for one of Paul's fast food trips)

A bar tab for forty-two dollars and twenty-four cents, paid in cash. *The Office.*

It wasn't the receipt that steamed Anna, nor the amount. She was fine with Paul going out with friends after work for drinks. And it wasn't the amount—Paul would call a cab before driving home drunk. It was the scribbled message on top: CALL ME, PAUL ♥ NIKKI, followed by a telephone number. A note from some floozy Paul met at the bar. *How long? How could he? Why …*

A million thoughts ran through her mind. A million questions. Anna had her suspicions, but the receipt finally drove them home.

"Allison, Peter!" Her voice cracked at the end of Peter's name. She cleared her throat.

"Breakfast!"

Her heart raced within her chest as she read the handwritten scribbles over and over again.

Paul. Nikki. The kids, they can never know. What should I say to Paul? Should I even confront Paul?

A million questions.

Fourteen years of marriage. The kids. Nikki. Paul.

A million thoughts, all at once.

Anna took the note and folded it in her hand, squeezed tight until her knuckles whitened. She used that fist to wipe her eyes dry, sniffed once and closed the wallet, which she placed into Paul's pocket where she'd found it. She crumpled the slacks within the rest of the load into the washer, set it on a full cycle, and walked away. Peter and Allison ran past her in the hallway.

She clenched the receipt, thought of her mother, thought of Lisa and the many fights they'd had over the years. She thought of the chest and remembered Lisa's doll and its cracked face, how she had buried it in the backyard all those years ago and how guilty she'd felt afterward. Mom always made things right; she had even helped unbury the doll in the middle of the night and later put it into the chest, the place to put things you wanted to forget.

Anna walked through the hallway to Peter's room. The chest was there, waiting, with its lid opened wide like a mouth ready to feast on bad memories. It seemed to pull her in, calling for her, calling for the scribbled note with Nikki's number. She fought tears and silenced the cries that wanted out of her. She had to be strong, like her mother. She read the note once more: CALL ME, PAUL ♥ NIKKI. Before tossing it into the chest, Anna's fingers ran over the phone number and her eyes to the phone on Peter's nightstand. She couldn't remember Peter having a phone in his room, but there it was.

Hands shaking, Anna reached for the phone and dialed. After a few agonizingly long rings, a familiar voice answered: "Hello?" It was Paul. A young woman's voice in the background said, "Who is it, honey?"

She shuddered and slammed the receiver down, tossed the receipt into the chest, and closed the lid.

Something kept Allison from sleeping, possibly the thunderstorm cracking light into her room every so often. The thunder was still a good seven seconds late from the lightning, according to Allison's count, but it was approaching steadily. Electric light illuminated her bedroom as she tangled within her sheets, slipping her pillow often to the cooler side, exposing her feet when she got too warm, and covering them when they grew cold. She couldn't get her mind off the chest.

How can things disappear? Can they?

"I bet it goes somewhere," her brother had said. "And wherever it goes, there's a big mound of treasure."

She sat up in bed. It was no use trying to sleep, not when her thoughts tried so madly to keep her awake …

Why didn't the flowers disappear?

Now it was her grandmother's voice filling her head, a voice she could barely remember at all, saying: *'cause there are some things you cannot forget, Allie.*

A much louder crack of thunder rattled the house.

She wondered if Peter was still awake, possibly organizing his next disappearing act, his next magic show. Maybe he'd even dress up a little and put on a red cape and black top hat.

Should we tell Mom?

Allison glanced to her own junk drawer and thought of the

many things she could make vanish.

Where does it all go?

Another loud clap, more distant.

I bet there's some place in the world where all this stuff ends up. And now it has Optimus on top, and my camo shirt, your dirty socks, and my Boggs rookie card.

Only Peter would come up with such a ludicrous thing to say. Yet, Optimus *had* vanished, Peter's camouflage shirt *had* vanished, her own wadded socks *had* vanished, and Boggs ...

She jumped out of bed, went to her dresser, and opened the top drawer. Wade Boggs stared up at her, a bat slung over his shoulder, his signature in black Sharpie. A few banded stacks from Peter's collection were next to it.

A loud thump sent a chill up her spine—not thunder, but a familiar sound: a chest lid. Peter playing magician.

He'll wake up Mom and ... well, probably just Mom.

Allison closed the drawer and headed to her brother's room to see for herself.

"Peter," she whispered as she entered, "what are you doing? You'll wake up the whole house." It sounded like something her mother would say.

"What're you putting in—"

Allison was alone.

Peter's bed was a mess, but that was nothing new. She poked her head out the door to look for the sliver of light coming from underneath the bathroom door, but he wasn't there, either. The entire house was a dark, hazy gray, lit sporadically with strobes of electric light. The thunder was nothing more than mild rumbles in the distance.

"Peter?"

Allison checked the other side of the bed in case the thump

she'd heard wasn't Peter rolling off in his slumber. But she knew the sound she'd heard.

Rain poured.

"Peter?"

She checked the chest, lifted its lid and found it empty. She searched the room again in case he was hiding—a simple prank, perhaps—but no Peter.

I bet it goes somewhere.

That's when she found the note Peter had left on his pillow for Allison to find. In childish scribble it read:

I went to find the
treshure. I'll be
back soon with my
Boggs card and you're
stupid socks.
        - Peter

Anna had been caught snoozing. She tried waiting up for Paul, but the heavy rain hypnotized her mind and pulled at her eyelids until she drifted to sleep. The sound of a door closing was her alarm and she instantly woke. She waited for the sound of Paul's keys to make contact with the end table, as well as the fridge opening, the microwave, the hiss of a beer or two before ready-ing for bed with not his lover, but his wife of fourteen years.

She waited with anticipation, but heard no such familiar—yet sickening to the heart—sounds.

Not the door?

"Paul," she whispered, and reached to his side of the bed; he wasn't there. The clock read 12:21 A.M.

Someone breaking into the house?

Her gut reaction told her to check on the kids. Her stomach knotted as she imagined a stranger with her sleeping children.

Rain attacked the window as lightning flashed. Anna counted out loud one-thousand-one to one-thousand-seven, before thunder rolled her out of bed and out of the room. She took an umbrella from the bucket next to the bedroom door. It wasn't to keep her dry, but to provide herself with a makeshift weapon. She held it like a bat, ready to swing.

Damn you, Paul. If you were home and not

(with ♥ NIKKI)

at The Office*, you'd be the one chasing bumps in the night and checking on the kids. Not me.*

"Sorry, honey, but my boss needs those expense reports by morning," Paul had told her that evening during dinner. "It should only take a few more hours. Don't wait up," he'd said. But she had waited until the rain sang her to sleep, until she heard the sound of a door slamming.

Maybe it wasn't the front door, but Peter closing the bathroom door a little too loudly. Maybe Peter had to pee. Maybe Peter—

wasn't in his room.

His light was off—which wasn't like Peter if he had to use the restroom in the middle of the night—and so was the bathroom light, Anna noticed. His room was a mess, but that was normal.

Anna lowered the umbrella as she headed to the bathroom and tapped the door gently with its tip.

"Peter?" She tapped a second time before opening the door and jumpstarting her heart with the reflection in the vanity mirror. She nearly dropped her weapon.

Pull yourself together, Anna. Those were the words of her mother, followed by her own: *Maybe Peter's in with Allison. A bad dream.*

Sometimes Peter would go to his sister after nightmares. Sometimes running from his room across to Allison's was easier than running to his parent's when the lights were out and the boogie-man was on the prowl.

Maybe Peter had a bad dream, got a little scared, and ran to his sister for comfort. Maybe Allison—

wasn't in her room, either.

She flipped on the lights and checked the giant mess of the comforter on the bed in case she and/or Peter were hidden underneath. She was about to call out Allison's name when she spotted her out the window, kneeling in the mud. She was digging with her hands deep into the ground, her hair sopping wet, her clothes drenched and clinging to her shivering skin.

Anna ripped Allison's comforter from the bed and bolted out of the room. She swung the door open and called to her daughter. Somewhere along the way, she dropped the umbrella.

"Allison!"

A crack of thunder worked as the exclamation point to her daughter's name, a flash of lightning before it.

Allison frantically dug with muddy fingers. The hole roughly the size of a shoebox. A stack of cards lay next to it, awaiting their burial.

"Allison," Anna yelled as she wrapped the comforter around her daughter, "what in the heavens are you doing?"

Allison continued her digging, her eyes tired and red.

"Where's your brother? Where's Peter?"

Allison's fingers clawed at the earth, her once dirty blonde hair now a muddy brown. "I was only trying to teach him a lesson. They didn't *really* disappear."

"Where's Peter?" Anna repeated.

"He went to find the treasure. He went to find Boggs but I had Boggs all along and my socks his shirt Optimus the water those other things too but not his autographed Boggs. Boggs is right here," she said, pushing the pile of cards into their grave, "with the other cards I took when he hadn't closed the lid yet to make him think they disappeared but they didn't disappear, they're right here." She pushed mounds of mud over them, sobbing between words. "But now they'll be gone and Peter won't ever find them."

The headlights from Paul's truck blinded Anna briefly as Paul rounded the corner of the driveway. Rain continued pouring, but she could still hear the crunching of gravel under the tires as he pulled into the driveway, the car door slamming shut, the gravel under his pattering feet.

And what is he thinking as he's running to aid them? Anna holding a wet comforter around their rocking daughter. Wade Boggs' muddy gravesite. Allison's messy fingers holding her black-streaked face. Peter, nowhere to be found.

Anna smelled the perfume on Paul—alcohol heavy on his breath—even through the storm.

Some things you cannot forget.

"Why didn't Grandma's flowers disappear?" Allison asked her. When we first found the chest, there were dead flowers inside … What if you don't want to forget the things you put inside?"

I remember I was eating a fried egg sandwich. I remember crying with food in my mouth.

"What's going on out here?" Paul asked. "Allison, let's get

you inside and cleaned up. *Honey? Where's Peter?"*

Anna said nothing. She rocked with her daughter. She knew the answer to his question. Peter was with the treasure. Peter was with Lisa's broken doll.

That same day I looked into the chest, to remember all the things I earlier wanted to forget.

Peter put himself into the chest, to remember all the things he earlier wanted to forget.

The chest was empty ...

"Except for the wilted flowers," mumbled Anna.

MOTH

With wings outstretched, I flutter majestic
Long I've traveled to find this light
Life: so humble and tragic
Flying upwards I fall
This glorious climb
Called depression
A way out
From doubt
Shout!
I bounce
It is glass
This sun of death
Displayed like a dream
Fool me once, fool me twice
You cannot trick me all night
Powdery wings or not, I'll fight
Until my body grows tired and folds

My form is weak, hallow and bristly
Long I've traveled to end this life
Light: so close and so costly
I tried to rise up from
This horrible fall
Called forgiveness
A way in
From sin
Pinned!
My wings
By needle
On crucifix
Displayed on a board
For all the world to see
This is not the end of me
Preserved body display beauty
With wings outstretched, I lay here majestic

WITHOUT FACE

"What did he look like?"

Cold. Criminal. Weathered. That was the alley. The single operational streetlight made the night air seem foggy, so that a flickering orange triangle sporadically lit and unlit Saul's sedan by the curb. High on whatever it was the stripper had shared with him, he stood on the sidewalk, dizzy, his surroundings swaying. The alley was empty. A lead pipe lay nearby; Saul thought of picking it up.

He could barely remember the club. Loud music. Hard Drinks. Skin. Vickie.

"It wasn't a man," he told the officer. Saul balanced the heavy load of his head within his grasp, elbows rubbing against his knees. The curb where he sat was wet. It had rained not long before all this happened. He sat in water.

She sat on his lap, as if waiting to hear a story. Her name was Vickie. A stage name. Her real name wasn't important. He wasn't paying for her real name; he was paying for Vickie.

"What's your name, stranger?" she asked, although she knew. "And why are you wearing a sweater, aren't you hot?"

"Saul."

"Saul. I like that." She brushed the back of her hand across his chest and sank further into his lap. She couldn't have weighed more than ninety pounds.

"Can you describe this person?" the officer asked.

"She was my height ... maybe five-ten. A hundred and fifty pounds, give or take. She wore black pajama pants and a white shirt with a crow on it. Slightly muscular."

"Do you work out?" asked the stripper, feeling Saul's flabby arms. It was a punch-card question, like "Is this your first time to a place like this?" or "Right here, or in the V.I.P. room?"

Saul snickered. "No. Not quite. You think I should?"

"Nah, you're fine just like this. It's all about how you feel that really matters."

"Are you feeling all right, mister ...?" the officer said, hunting for more information to add to his notebook.

"Pravat. Saul Pravat."

"You look a bit flushed, Mr. Pravat." Out came the mini-flashlight.

"I feel fine," Saul said. "Really, I am fine."

"Stand up. Let me take a look at your eyes."

"You have the most amazing eyes," he said to Vickie.

In the comfort of the V.I.P. room, she straddled him wearing nothing but a few strings and some triangular cloth.

"Do I?" she asked, batting her eyelashes flirtatiously. "Usually my customers focus their attention elsewhere." Off came her sorry excuse for a bra. She slid it over Saul's face before placing it around his neck.

Still, her eyes held him.

"You're a strange man, you know that?"

He smiled and shrugged.

"What?" she laughed.

"Nothing. It's just … they're so twitchy," he said, meaning her eyes; he watched as they bounced back and forth, focusing alteratively between his own. Left. Right. Left.

Vickie covered her face and blushed. "You caught me," she said and laughed again. "I've got a secret. Promise not to tell?"

"You're on something."

"You want in?" It was more of an understanding.

"You should know me better than that. You can't even remember my name, and you've danced for me how many times?"

"Seven. Now close your eyes and open up."

"Have you been taking any drugs, Mr. Pravat?" the officer asked as he blasted a beam of light into Saul's eyes.

"Yes, sir."

"What kind?"

"I'm not sure, sir," Saul said, like one sloshed word: shurser.

"Have you also been drinking, Mr. Pravat?"

❧

"You haven't had a load to drink tonight, right?" Vickie asked, fingers paused mid-flight to her secret stash.

Jaw gaped, Saul peeked between squeezed eyelids and caught a glimpse of her "stash" before closing them and saying, "Just a few sissy drinks, nothing special."

Soon Saul tasted Vickie's finger and whatever bitter-chalky drug she gave him.

Loud music filled his ears, the bass thumping and thumping, a naked treasure dancing and grinding against him to the beat. He opened his eyes and the world around him spun.

On the other side of the room, another dancer was "dancing" on another's lap; next to him sat a lonely woman roughly the same size as Saul. She wore black pajama pants and a white shirt with a crow etched on front, her knees pointing to Saul, hands in her lap.

She didn't have a face.

"Can you explain the blood on your shirt?"

To Saul, the officer's words were spoken in a contorted slow-motion. Intense nausea forced Saul to purge his drug and alcohol intake onto his slacks and shoes. Some landed on the man asking the questions.

"Are you okay?" Vickie asked. "You look sick."

The woman without a face stared back, although she had no eyes with which to stare. She in fact held no such facial features; she had smooth skin where a face should reside.

The stripper and guy next to this faceless woman didn't seem to notice her presence; the woman on top continued slithering to the beat.

The woman without a face rose.

Saul fell to the ground. "She didn't have a face," he said.

"She doesn't have a face," Saul said casually.

"What?" Vickie asked.

"That lady doesn't have a face." He started to shake.

"Who?"

Saul pointed an edgy finger.

Vickie twisted around. "That's Julie, with a customer. You're with me now." She held his face in her petite hands and smiled.

"You don't look well. Maybe you should get some water."

He swatted her hands away as the faceless woman took a step closer.

Vickie slapped him. Hard. Red lines highlighted his cheekbone.

The faceless woman took another step, hands at her side. And then she took another.

Saul jumped from the black V.I.P. couch, launching Vickie to the ground in a crumpled mess. Her wrist snapped.

"Get away from me!" he screamed.

"Sir, I am going to have to ask you to calm down. Where did the blood on your shirt come from, Mr. Pravat?"

"Get away from me!"

"Sir, are you injured? Is this blood yours? I need you to calm down, sir." The officer radioed for assistance.

A lead pipe smashed into his skull. The sound was solid, quick, metallic. His eyes went blank. His head leaked crimson oil. He collapsed to the ground in front of Saul.

In the officer's place stood the woman without a face. She dropped the pipe. Held her arms out. A stretched skin replaced all facial features on this woman. The crow on her shirt, a silhouette, perched solemnly with its mouth open, ready to swallow. It had fiery red eyes.

Saul screamed.

"Get the hell away from me!"

The others in the club stirred. Vickie, injured, lay confused on the tiled floor. Julie and her dance partner stared from the opposite couch. Another woman wearing skimpy apparel peeked around the doorway.

The woman without a face stretched out her arms, palms up, and continued to close the short distance.

The ground beneath Saul was like tarp covered with water, the drugs taking effect. The room spun. He almost tumbled to the door. Soft fingers grabbed his shoulder. *Her* fingers. She spun him around but he closed his eyes, hoping to make her go away.

The officer lay facedown as the faceless stranger approached. Saul closed his eyes.

The hold on his shoulder was piercing. Opening his eyes, he found himself facing one of the club bouncers, who stood nearly a foot taller than Saul, and outweighed him close to double.

Vickie was crying on the floor. The others in the club glared. Everyone had red eyes like the crow; they glowed eerily in the dark V.I.P. room. The drugs, perhaps.

"Where is she?" Saul shouted. "Where is she?"

"You threw her to the floor. Get out of here!" The bouncer grabbed Saul by the armpits and dragged him out of the small room. Saul's button-up sweater slowly ripped open, revealing a shirt covered in blood.

"You saw her, Vickie," Saul pleaded. "Tell him. Tell him you saw the woman without a face! Tell him!"

He looked around frantically to find her, but she was gone.

The room paused for Vickie's response.

"Get that bastard out of here. He's delusional and whacked on drugs." She held her broken wrist. "There was no such woman."

She stood above Saul, expressionless, emotionless, featureless.

A pool of blood surrounded the downed officer, forming from the wide gash at the back of his head. He was dead.

The faceless woman held her hands out to Saul and took another step forward, and kicked the lead pipe she had dropped; it rolled within reaching distance. She leaned over Saul and softly put a hand onto his. She leaned in closer. Closer …

With his free hand, Saul felt for the pipe. Found it with his fingertips. Took it. Swung it into her faceless head. He shook his other hand free from hers. She fell over onto her side and landed next to the officer. A gushing slice in her otherwise smooth face pulsed black sludge. Not red, but black and viscous like molasses. Still, she reached for him as he stood on wobbly legs.

He lifted the lead pipe high into the air, ready to bring it down.

In bed, Cathy reached out for her husband and found a shaky hand. The clock on her nightstand revealed it was a few minutes past midnight. Another nightmare for her husband it would seem. She could barely distinguish his shape in the dark room but could tell he was sitting upright. Saul often woke from nightmares in the middle of the night. Cathy had it in her mind these dreams were brought on by guilt. She knew Saul frequented strip clubs; she could smell it on him. She also knew Saul probably knew she knew.

"Another nightmare, honey?"

Saul kept quiet.

"Saul?"

No response.

She thought of asking who Vickie was, but thought better of it. He sometimes mentioned that name during restless sleep. Instead she reached over and switched on the lamp at her side.

Saul was thrown out the door by the bouncer. He landed hard onto the ground a few steps away. His sweater lay loosely draped over his shoulders, a few buttons torn free.

Hurt, confused, drugged and drunk, Saul staggered along the sidewalk. He headed to his car but quickly diverted down a nearby alley to throw up, hoping the woman without a face wouldn't follow. He saw a lead pipe near the mess he made, thought of picking it up, but decided not to.

The sound of a kicked can in the black depths of the alley jumpstarted Saul's heart. He waited a moment, shaking uncontrollably. He knew it was her, the woman without a face. She was reaching for him in the darkness.

The dumpster rolled as something on the other side leaned against it. And then he saw her as she slapped the side of the dumpster with a wet hand.

Saul ran.

Saul waited for Cathy to reach for the lamp at her side. He wanted to be sure.

She did so after calling out his name. The light came on. She turned his way. She didn't have a face.

Saul straddled his wife and brought the lead pipe down over and over again. His shirt soaked in spatters of blood. He continued swinging until he was unable to discern a face of any kind. After a moment, the only way Saul was able to tell it had been Cathy was her nightshirt. He had given her the shirt with the crow on it years ago. She often wore it to bed.

Saul washed his hands and face, put on a button-up sweater, and walked out the door.

"Slow down, sir," said the officer.

Saul was unable to breathe. He had nearly run the officer over bolting from the alley. He was hyperventilating.

"Chasing … me!"

"Who is chasing you, sir?"

What followed was a series of uncaught breaths.

"Why is your shirt covered in blood? Are you hurt?"

"Chasing me!" Saul said between collected gasps of air.

"Slow down," the officer said, trying to illustrate the art of breathing with simple hand gestures.

"What did he look like?"

THE BOX

Set down on my porch
A small brown box
Inside, I don't know
It could be for me
Or someone else
Perhaps placed by mistake
No address
To or from
A sealed cardboard container
About nine inches cubed
Shaken, something within
Thuds around
Quite heavily

An unknown mass
Raising intrigue and curiosity
As I toss it to the floor
Should this box be replaced
Back onto my porch
For someone else to find
Shall I just open it
A knife would do justice
To slice apart the tape
And I could peek inside
If only I had eyes
But they're back with my head
Which I misplaced long ago

THE SHOWER CURTAIN MAN

He's the guy you see on the street corner holding a sign that reads: NEED HELP. The letters are crooked and so are his teeth and he has this blank expression on his face. It isn't hunger. He isn't asking for food. He's not asking for money or gas and he wasn't in a war or looking for a job. His sign is a torn flap of cardboard box and the words are written in either shit or dried blood. He's asking for help and he's a guy just like me.

I saw him three days in a row during my lunch breaks. He was always in that same spot, always holding the same sign. All the lettering was capitalized except for the d, I remember that much, and he wore the same clothes one day to the next: sun-bleached holey jeans, a long-sleeved red shirt starting to turn pink, and flip-flop sandals. His hair was short but matted, like that of a stray dog. The rest of the man was clean and his face recently shaven; either that, or he was incapable of growing facial hair. He wasn't thin, by any means, but his sign didn't tell me he was hungry the day I decided to roll down my window; it told me he needed help.

He didn't look at me. He wasn't looking at anything; his eyes were lost to the world around him. I knew if I got out of the car and waved a hand in his face he wouldn't see me.

No one was behind me when the light at the intersection turned green, so I put the car in Park and leaned out the window.

I held out a ten-dollar bill—what I was going to use to buy my lunch. He seemed to need it more than I did.

"Hey, buddy."

The man rocked on his heels. He didn't make a move for the money and it was then I assumed he was blind. His eyes were a bit frosted over, similar to an animal losing its sight. Perhaps he was deaf, too, because he didn't budge when I called out to him a second time, or even when I banged against the side of the door.

And then I did what any sane man wouldn't have done in my scenario; I got out of the car and approached him. Luckily the street was dead; otherwise I would have pissed off a number of people. I held the money out as if the man were rabid and about to bite. He looked through me, even as I inched closer.

"Sir, I have some money. There are a number of fast food joints down the street. You could buy some food, or something to drink. Lunch is on me today."

His breath was rotten oranges.

Up close, he appeared to be in his mid-thirties, his skin dried out and a few years older because of the sun. His teeth were spotlessly white for a homeless fellow and he didn't appear to be missing any; I could see nearly all of them with his mouth dangling open. I watched as spittle dropped from his bottom lip and fell to the ground at his feet. He needed help. The sign wasn't lying.

One of his pockets contained a whitish handkerchief that was trying to escape; his other pocket appeared empty, but I didn't dare place the bill inside, fearing for how the strange man might react. Instead, I jimmied the folded ten-dollar bill in between his fingers and the makeshift sign.

"Take it easy," I said to him, returning to the car.

When the light changed a second time, I drove away and saw him in the rearview mirror. He didn't seem to notice the money I had given him and he didn't wave as I had expected; he simply stared at my taillights, or perhaps at my reflection in the mirror.

He wasn't there the following day, or the next. I wasn't planning to give him more money, but after seeing even a stranger standing at a street corner for three days in a row, you miss him when he's gone.

I wonder sometimes if he ever saw me driving away that day, or what he thought of me for getting out of the car to give him the money. I called him 'buddy,' but part of me wanted to know his name, to know that he was once a normal guy, like me, not some half-baked bum on the streets begging for loose change, a hobo walking alone in some kind of figurative darkness only he could understand. Had he experienced life? Had he ever loved? Maybe he had those things once—what we take for granted—and they threw him away—to the curb no less—where I found him.

A woman was holding his sign on that same street corner the following week. She had used a permanent marker to scratch out the word HELP and replaced it with MONEY. Underneath those words she had scribbled GOD BLESS, with both of the S's drawn backward. It was a gimmick, I knew. Most of the homeless could spell, but used misspellings so dopes like me would feel sorrier for them. Little did this woman know, gods didn't give a shit about her; if they did, she'd have a place to call home, a job, or at least some money of her own to hand out to strangers living off the street, to people like her.

I rolled down my window after stopping at the light and leaned my head out.

"Where'd you get the sign?"

"Huh?"

"The sign. Where'd you get it?"

"I found it. It's mine." She coughed into her hand and held that same hand out to me, begging. "Can you spare some money god bless?" It was a well-rehearsed line she spurted out.

I grabbed what little change I could find and held it out to her. The car honking behind me startled us both. A black Suburban filled my rearview mirror. The light had turned green and the person behind me had turned impatient.

The lady shook her head disapprovingly.

"I don't want no change," she said.

"Here," I said, starting to roll forward. "Take it."

"A few dollars?" she asked again, a beggar with high standards, it seemed.

The Suburban honked twice, short but not threatening. It was then I noticed what else the homeless woman had scrawled onto the sign: $2. She wanted cash, and a set amount.

As I continued to roll forward, she followed me.

"Tell me where you got your sign and I'll give you a ten. There was a guy here last week holding that sign. Have you seen him?"

"Only a few dollars," the hag said. She was holding onto the door now. "Just a few dollars god bless."

Her teeth were covered in yellow and brown slime and she smelled like a sour mix of whiskey and beef jerky. Her fingernails could probably scratch the paint, they were so overgrown and crusty. For a split second, she resembled the evil witch from Snow White, but instead of holding out a poisoned apple, she held out her hand for a set amount—two bucks.

Disgusted, I sped off. In the side-view mirror, the miniature homeless woman was no longer interested in me; she was walking to the next car in line, holding the stolen sign.

I took a long shower before going to bed that night and stood there with the water raining onto the back of my head. I couldn't get him out of my mind: that blank stare, the flakes of dandruff on his shoulders, the sun-bleached red shirt that was starting to turn pink. Even after I had given him the money, he hadn't budged. He just stood there with his sign. NEED HELP. The poor fellow didn't want to work for food; he wasn't hard up for liquor; he wasn't even drenched in filth like the lady after him—the lady who had somehow gotten ahold of his sign. Was he still on the streets? Was he dead? For some unknown reason, I cared.

Sleep overtook me a little after eleven. I remember rolling around uncomfortably for a while, opening my eyes once to read 11:34 on the alarm clock before closing them again. I dreamt about him and I remember the dream well.

The gold band around my finger let me know I was married again. June had left me years ago, but in the dream I was still married to her. We were running through some kind of dead field and at the end of the field was a wooden fence, which we sat on to pick out the burrs from our socks. We were happy and laughing, but I don't remember why. All I remember is seeing the guy from the street corner watching us from not too far away; only his upper half was visible over the grain, but I could tell it was him. "Who is that?" June had asked, her voice no longer happy. She shook as she pointed to him. The man in the field had glowing blue eyes; even in broad daylight they burned like dwarf stars, and they were difficult to turn away from, as if they were the deadlights from that book about the evil clown. "I don't know," I lied to her, but I knew who he was; he was a nobody I saw during my lunch breaks … before he suddenly disappeared; he was the guy I gave ten bucks to once, whether he knew it or not. He wore the same battered holey jeans, the same long-sleeved, once-red shirt. His feet were buried in the field, but I knew they'd be wearing flip-flop sandals. He stood there menacingly. Some kind of demonic statue. A monster.

I woke trembling when something in the house crashed to the floor. The clock next to me glowed eerily blue, which made me think of the eyes in the dream. It was a quarter after two in the morning. The rest of the bedroom remained blanketed in darkness. I figured I had knocked over the glass on my nightstand during my sleep, but when I felt for it, it was there; after turning on the lamp, so was he.

The man from the street corner stood next to my bed. He had those empty, glazy eyes. They were blue, but a blue as light as the sky over Los Angeles. He held a toilet plunger in one hand, as if he were going to strike me with it. He was naked underneath the clear plastic shower curtain wrapped around his body—the shower curtain from my own bathroom. The man was soaked from head to toe. He didn't shiver, but the flesh on his arms was covered in gooseflesh, almost reptilian. Water trailed behind him and led to the door leading out of the bedroom. Crumpled within his other hand was the ten-dollar bill I had given him. I knew that because someone had defaced the bill by drawing a cigarette dangling from Hamilton's mouth.

I should have been lost for words, but I somehow managed to say, "I looked for you. The—the next day, I looked for you and you were gone. I wanted to see you there, on the street corner, to see if you were alright."

He didn't say anything, but leaned over me and dripped water onto my face as he held the toilet plunger. Behind him,

I heard the shower running. I pictured him standing in the tub with cold water raining over him, plunger in hand. Now he stood over me, the plunger held high over his head.

He stuck it hard against the wall. His eyes never left mine. It made a comical *pthunk* sound, but neither of us laughed. A picture on the wall fell to the floor, and it was the same sound as before. I finally broke his gaze. A ring of water ran down the wall behind him near the door. Another framed picture lay broken on the floor beneath it. The sound that woke me was a framed picture crashing against the floor. It held a picture of me and June two years prior, back when we were married. It was one of my favorites because we were both smiling. I had hung it on the bedroom wall closest to the door so I'd see it every day when leaving for work, to remind myself that there was still love in the world.

He glanced from me to the wall as he tried to pull the plunger free, but it was stuck. The wadded bill in his other hand fell to the ground as he pulled hard on the handle. The wall bowed with each tug. He brought his other hand up to help and the shower curtain fell, exposing his nudity, as well as his sexual arousal. His member stood at attention, his boys tucked in close. Eventually he gave in to the plunger; it stuck straight out, like him. He retrieved the fallen currency, smiled, and then set it back on the floor. And then he walked out of my life forever, leaving me with this strange story to tell others.

Why this strange man was walking around in my house in the middle of the night sticking a plunger against my bedroom walls, I will never know, nor will I ever know how or when he followed me home, or why he was naked, wet and wearing my clear plastic shower curtain as a means of clothing.

I called the police and told them what had happened. They

sent an officer over to investigate, but it took him over fifteen minutes to get to the house, so I spent that time locking all the windows and doors. I never found the man's clothes. He either grabbed them on his way out, or had arrived buck naked. I turned off the shower, sat on the edge of my bed and stared absentmindedly at the money he had oddly returned. I glanced every so often to the erect plunger sticking out from my wall. I could still smell the rotten orange on his breath, long after he left, and long after the officer had taken my statement and wished me a pleasant morning. I think of him every time I drink orange juice.

Throughout the weekend, I was a recluse, peeking out the windows every once in a while to see if he would return. I called the police department a few times to see if they found him, but they didn't seem to care. They never found him. For all they knew, he probably never existed. All they had was my story about the shower curtain man. They probably thought I was crazy.

Monday morning I drove to work. I took all the same routes and when I got to my street corner, the old homeless hag was waiting for me with her sign. $2 was crossed out; it now read $10. I rolled down my window and gave her the money I was going to use for lunch, the crumpled bill with the smoking Hamilton. She smiled a set of crooked teeth. With alcohol still on her breath, she said, "Just a few dollars god bless."

STRANGERS

A stranger came without knocking
He was silent
A stealth-like invisible ghost
And he was lone

The stranger had unique style
Clashing badly
With colors, 'never knew I had
Of white and red

The stranger invited some friends
For a party
Of nomadic wandering speed
And they lingered

The strangers decided to stay
Never leaving
Mixing their paints on my canvas
Turning me gray

The strangers tested my patience
Making a mess
My life forever invaded
With new changes

And then the strangers just left me
Empty and cold
They cannot come back, not ever
My body folds

FIX

The last time Gabriel Lane saw his wife she was dead and naked on a ruffled bed at Freemont Motel off Freemont Street. A needle stuck from the pockmarked crease where her forearm met her bicep, heroin oozing near the tip like milk, her veins dark and swollen. Matted blonde hair covered half her face. The other half revealed a cloudy dead eye.

Why would you do this to me, Gabriel?

She was dead, but had somehow said this to him. He grabbed the black balloon at her side and left her cold body for the police.

"Will the room be for one, or for two, sir?"

"Two," Gabriel said to the man behind the counter. He slid him a credit card. "I'm sorry. One. Only one."

The hotel was paradise compared to Freemont and the lobby smelled of lilac.

"How many nights will you be staying?"

The question caught him off guard. He needed a quiet room to help him concentrate on writing, not his life. He had had enough of the investigations, the therapy, the rehabilitation. Amber dying on him was in the past, but it seemed the more he tried to forget her death, the more it ate at his writing. Screenplays didn't write themselves. If Gabriel couldn't produce a first draft in seven days, the studio would either cancel the project, or hire a new hand to write the script.

"Is there a weekly rate?"

The man at the counter pointed to a printout that listed room rates. He moved his finger below an amount. "Take that number, and multiply it by the number of nights you will be staying."

"*No* would have been fine," said Gabriel. "Reserve the room for the rest of the week."

"Will there be anything else, sir?"

Gabriel didn't answer. He took the keycard and carried his bags to 196, a tidy room that smelled of cleaning solvents and cigarette smoke. Unlike the room at Freemont, the bed was made, the carpet vacuumed, and there weren't any scurrying cockroaches.

Gabriel cleared the welcome information from the top of the desk and setup his workspace. He slapped his notepad down and set a few pens around it. Next to it he placed a box of rounded toothpicks, his replacement for heroin. He broke three over empty lines of paper before retiring to bed.

The lights were off, but the television hummed on; it had turned on by itself, Gabriel nearly dreaming. The room flashed scenery over the walls. The volume muted. At first, Gabriel thought he had rolled on top of the controller, but it sat on top of the set.

As he watched the silent screen, he couldn't help but fill in the script to give it life. It was an old habit that used to drive Amber crazy. Amber was always the one with the remote, but he'd sometimes take it from her and turn down the sound. He'd describe the film to her in manuscript form, setting the scenery, the dialogue, everything. Sometimes he'd do it to piss her off and she'd cuss the living fuck out of him.

Gabriel wasn't sure why the television had turned on. Perhaps the maid had swapped remotes during services with the room next door. He watched and setup the scene:

INT. LIVING ROOM - EARLY MORNING

A crowded coffee table contains everything but cups of coffee. A brownish-green mix of water in a half-filled glass holds paint brushes. Next to it is an unfinished rectangle of canvas over wood illustrating this exact scene, including the razor blade and lines of cocaine waiting on a mirrored coaster.

The canvas does not, however, show JANE or JOHN DOE, who are both sitting on a brown leather sofa overlooking the coffee table.

Soft morning light fills the otherwise dark room through mini-blinds in the adjacent kitchen. Clothing and trash litter the carpet.

JOHN reaches for a rolled billfold on the floor. He leans forward and snorts a line of white from the glass.

JANE looks to him with disgust. She starts to grab a corner of the canvas, but her hand is swatted away as one might brush off lint.

> JOHN DOE
> It's not even dry. You'll smear
> it.

> JANE DOE
> I'm not going to smear it. What
> is there to smear? You've only
> started the middle. What is it?
> Us? It's the damn coffee table.

JOHN'S eyes are bloodshot spider webs. Paint-covered fingers rub his nose as he sniffs at what sounds like an oncoming cold or sinus congestion.

> JANE DOE (CONCERNED)
> You need to stop this.

> JOHN DOE
> The painting?

> JANE DOE
> The drugs. The paintings. All
> of it. Look at you! You're
> twitching. You can't even hold
> a brush still. When was the
> last time you—

> JOHN DOE
> You like it?

                    JANE DOE
          It's our fucking coffee table …

Leaning over the coffee table, JOHN snorts the
last line of cocaine from the coaster. He throws
the billfold to the carpet and sinks into the
sofa, his arms stretched wide. He knocks over an
empty beer bottle, which clangs against the leg
of the table. He breathes deeply, as if taking
his last breath.

                    JOHN DOE
              It's unbelievable, this feel-
              ing. This feeling of recursive
              ecstasy. God, you have to try
              this shit!

                JANE DOE (SARCASTIC)
              Wow. Yes. Good shit. Can't wait
              to try it. Oh, look. It's gone.

Abruptly, JOHN leans forward in his seat.

Rage replaces paranoia as he backhands JANE's
face.

JANE is knocked backward. Tears well in her eyes.
One of her own hands finds its way to the swelling
red cheek.

JOHN wets his index finger and rubs it over the

mirrored coaster. With his free hand, he grabs
JANE by the throat and forces the cocaine laden
finger into her mouth.

                                        FADE OUT:

Gabriel's push had been heroin. For most of his writing career, it was the needle that gave birth to his ideas. His art: born from the push. Sometimes, when he shot up, he'd get a rush of inspiration. Amber would be there to watch him. She'd get that concerned look on her face that pissed him off. She'd watch him, but she wouldn't join in the fun.

One time he gave her a script to read—some pilot about a group of friends finding faith in each other—and she didn't seem to like it. She laughed, but it wasn't a comedy. Gabriel had hit her, hard. It was the heroin. He knew it now. When she finally stopped crying, it was because she had fallen asleep. He had cuddled next to her and shot her with heroin.

He never told Amber what he did to her. She woke up the next morning and puked her guts out. She ran a fever and wrapped herself in a blanket. Gabriel spent that day rewriting the pilot. He shot up twice and finished a sixth and final draft before they ate dinner. He asked Amber to read it over. She kept rubbing her arm as she read the manuscript, not laughing as she had before. She said she liked it and that it was ready to go out. He eventually sold the script, but the project got canned.

A week after he hit her, she didn't mind him shooting up all the time. She seemed more interested in his work than his work habits. He remembered the exact time—11:11—and the exact date—February the 29th—when Amber transformed. She was no longer the sweet, innocent Amber Lane.

The needle was still in Gabriel's arm when she took it from him. She took the needle away. She took the black magic balloon away. He watched, stoned, as Amber took it all away, and then used it on herself. She shot up, a look of relief on her face. She sat with him on the couch a while. They had made love, or perhaps the opposite.

Gabriel came to and left the television muted as the show re-turned. It got his creative juices flowing. He setup the scene:

EXT. A CITY PARK - EVENING

Wind rolls fallen leaves and debris across a dying playground. The seats of a rusty swing set sway as if ridden, but the children are gone. The chains creak softly. Sawdust underneath hold puddles of murky water where feet have eroded the ground.

A condom floats unwrapped in the leftmost puddle, an empty beer can next to it. They dance together in the water.

                                        FADE TO:

INT. MOTEL ROOM - EVENING

A queen-sized bed with a horridly patterned comforter fills most of the motel room, and is anything but comforting. The once white walls are water-damaged. Cracked artwork of a woman riding a horse hangs crooked above the headboard. An alarm clock on the night stand flips to 7:31 P.M.

In her underwear, JANE DOE sits at the edge the bed. Her black bra holds on by a single strap with the other dangling off her slumped shoulder. Dark rings bury her eyes. She stares forward, seemingly at nothing. At her side is a Bible with razor cuts of white powder on the cover, and JOHN, passed out on his back.

                                        CUT TO:

INT. THE OTHER SIDE OF THE MOTEL ROOM - EVENING

A dark glass television screen reveals JANE staring at herself. She watches her reflection wipe tears from her face. She fixes her fallen bra strap and reaches for the cocaine.

                    JANE DOE
          It's unbelievable, this feel-
          ing. This feeling of recursive
          ecstasy.

JANE'S reflection brings the Bible to her nose. She sniffs deeply. Her eyes roll upward as long-awaited relief fills her face. Blood trickles from one nostril. Her eyes climb into her head before she falls next to JOHN.

CUT TO:

INT. MOTEL ROOM - HOURS LATER

An alarm clock on the stand reads 3:42 A.M. Lamp-
light fills the small room. JANE and JOHN DOE lay
next to each other on the ruffled bed.

JOHN stirs, stretches, yawns. One of his legs
nudges JANE, but she doesn't move. He sits in
bed, puts a hand on her hip.

JANE is peaceful, curled like a newborn. She is
naked, except for the black satin bra and pant-
ies.

JOHN moves his hand gently along her side and to
the nape of her neck. He leans in and caresses
her there before slipping a strap off her shoulder. He kisses her again, but she doesn't move.
With his other hand, JOHN grabs the black satin
archway at her hips and pulls the material to her
ankles.

The television hummed off, leaving Gabriel in the dark. A green
shape stayed behind on the screen and slowly disappeared as he
searched the room blindly. He knocked his keys to the floor, and
nearly the lamp. The alarm clock on his nightstand read 3:43
A.M. in bright red numbers. Gabriel used its eerie light to try the
lamp, but the lamp only clicked when he twisted the knob.

Amber filled his mind. The thought of her dead body next to him all those years ago in Freemont Motel, like Jane from the movie, but overdosing on heroin instead of cocaine. The thought of making love to her in that condition, either dead or on her way to meet Death. The thought of that cloudy dead eye staring at him.

Why would you do this to me, Gabriel?

Amber killed herself. The police report had it written as an accidental drug overdose. Amber's first time was Gabriel's doing. He had raped her … not with his body, but with his needle. Soon after that, she began raping herself. Both had fucked with the drug, and the drug had fucked back.

A red-illuminated emptiness enveloped him. He kept expecting Amber's cold hand to cover his own.

Gabriel closed his eyes, but her dead stare—burned into his subconscious—continued to watch him through the matted blonde hair covering her face.

Her black corpse lips, ever so parted, would soon ask *Why would you do this to me, Gabriel?* with rotted breath. She'd nakedly straddle his body—ribs showing through her chest, a syringe sticking from one of her boney bruised arms like the hilt of a knife—and she'd whisper his name, leaning into him. Before making love, they'd shoot up together.

And when they'd wake the following morning, she'd take that knife he stabbed her with five years ago and begin stabbing herself with it until she bled out.

Somewhere on the nightstand was the box of toothpicks. His fingers frantically intertwined. He pried his fingers apart—risking Amber's touch—and felt for the box—his new push—and found them. Gabriel took two. He put one in his mouth and let the other flip between his knuckles.

His mind eased. Amber no longer sat over him. He was again alone in room 196.

The television hummed on. Gabriel hadn't realized he had fallen asleep until the soft noise startled him awake. The room once again flickered hard against his tired eyes with life of light and shadow.

"Why would you do this to me?" said a woman's voice.

Shivers ran along Gabriel's spine.

The question came from Jane Doe, her body ineptly positioned on the bed with John standing over her. She was completely naked on screen. A pair of glazed eyes gazed into the camera. Red ran from her nostrils and along her cheek, a mess of cocaine and blood. She had died smiling.

"Why would you do this to me?" she said without moving her lips. It was one of those cheesy voice-overs from the grave.

Gabriel noticed the bag of coke next to her. So did his John Doe on the screen; he snatched it and walked out the door.

As the scene ended, Gabriel took over the script:

CUT TO:

INT. HOTEL LOBBY – AFTERNOON

An UPTIGHT MAN IN HOTEL GARB looks down his nose to JOHN DOE as he stands behind an oversized maple counter. He types noisily on the keyboard next to him.

JOHN searches his pockets for his wallet. The paint covering his kakis presents a rainbow of color. A few rips in his pant legs show skin beneath. His buttoned shirt is clean, but wrinkled. A few splotches of paint clumps his hair.

> UPTIGHT MAN IN HOTEL GARB
> How many nights will you be stay-ing?

JOHN scratches his head and reaches into his shirt pocket for a pack of cigarettes. He pulls one free, holds it between his fingers and looks at it longingly.

> UPTIGHT MAN IN HOTEL GARB
> There is no smoking in here, sir.

> JOHN DOE
> Sorry. I know. It calms me sometimes just holding one of these cancer sticks. You know— old habits die hard or some shit.

> UPTIGHT MAN IN HOTEL GARB
> How many nights?

> JOHN DOE
> Right. Sorry. Um—

JOHN DOE reads the name badge on the man's uniform:
ASST. HOTEL MANAGER.

> JOHN DOE (CONTINUED)
> Is there some kind of weekly
> rate? I'm kinda tight on money
> and not sure how long I need
> to be here. I'm sketching a
> series of—

> ASST. HOTEL MANAGER
> I'm sure it's wonderful. Here
> are the rates for this hotel.

The ASST. HOTEL MANAGER slides a sheet of paper
in front of JOHN and points to it with his finger.

> ASST. HOTEL MANAGER
> Take that number and multiply
> it by the number of nights you
> will be staying.

"List me for the week," finished Gabriel.

A moment later, those same words were repeated by his scraggly counterpart on screen. The room numbers even matched, Gabriel realized, as a key tagged 196 was passed across the counter.

Gabriel pinched his arm, but he wasn't dreaming. He was watching his life played out on television. Gabriel Lane was John Doe and John Doe was Gabriel Lane. Jane Doe was his wife, his dead wife Amber. The uptight assistant hotel manager was the same asshole he'd talked to that afternoon when first checking into his room. The same fucking room, even.

He reached for his toothpicks on the nightstand and knocked them to the floor. The box rattled as it hit the carpet. He heard his fix scatter. He thought of a decayed Amber waiting underneath his bed and hesitated before grabbing one. He felt her dried skin as he leaned over the side, but realized he had brushed against one of his leather shoes. As Gabriel flipped a stick between his knuckles, the setting changed on the screen.

The television showed John Doe at a hotel room desk, an unlit cigarette dangling from his mouth, seemingly taunted by a blank sketchpad. A few sheets were crumpled on the floor. His hands shook. The movie moved to the next scene:

                                              CUT TO:

INT. HOTEL ROOM - EARLY MORNING

Light from an alarm clock paints the room red. It reads 4:24 A.M. and reflects reversely off the blank television screen.
The room is dark, but bright enough to reveal JOHN DOE sleeping on his back, fully dressed. His feet point to the ceiling, his chest rising and falling with drawn-out breaths.

The drone of a violin drowns JOHN'S slumber, intensifies as a second person in the room synchronously rises from the foot of the bed.

Wet black hair covers half of JANE DOE'S rotted face as a single blank eye stares at him. Her skin glows crimson with the room. Black sludge leaks from her nostrils. Brittle arms reach out like the appendages of a spider. They bend in awkward angles as they pull her naked form over the corner of the bed and on top of him. She is ravenous. Her sunken stomach and exposed ribcage reveal her hunger. Her bare legs straddle JOHN as sharp nails pull at the waistline of his pants, cutting deep as she instinctually grinds her lower half against him.

As JOHN wakes from his stupor, JANE grabs his throat and makes the opposite of love with him.

The television hummed off. Gabriel Lane turned to the red numbers of the alarm clock on his nightstand. The time changed from 4:23 to 4:24 A.M. His reflection in the blank television screen was ever so haunting as he waited for Amber to rise from the edge of the bed.

THE HAND

Clouds part and down falls a hand
Thunder crackles with static
Legs weak, unable to stand
Mankind falls down erratic

This is not the end of life
Nor the beginning of death
It's only God with his knife
Slicing your guilty last breath

Some it will gut from within
Others may run off to hide
But one cannot forfeit sin
When the hand crosses our side

Now is the time to pick right
When the rest of us choose wrong
Look between the clouds to light
Listen for the angels' song

Search for the hand in the sky
Lest it be coming for you
Then kneel on your knees to cry
For it will cut you in two

GOLDEN RULE

He wore the trench coat to the table and after sorting through a duffle bag next to him on the seat, he zipped the bag closed and smiled to the waiter, who seemed eager for the coat.

"I'm coldblooded, but thank you. I'd rather leave it on."

Still the waiter with the towel draped over his arm would not leave. He placed a basket of oily breadsticks onto the table. A dish of black-speckled olive oil lay next to it for dipping. He grabbed a metal device from the pouch in his apron and scraped fallen breadcrumbs from the tablecloth.

"Would you care to hear the specials?"

"I'm waiting for the rest of my party, an overweight fellow with a fifth-grade haircut. He looks like a child molester and will be wearing a brown pullover with black chinos. And he should be alone. Can you send him this way when he arrives?"

He pushed a twenty across the table.

The waiter slid the bill into his apron with practiced elegance.

"My name is Anthony and I will be happy to bring you this man." He made it sound as if he would bring the man's head on a platter for a set amount.

"Would you care for wine?"

He held an empty wine glass between his index and middle fingers and balanced it expectantly.

"Bring me a bottle of Cabernet. Your most expensive."

"Our most expensive bottle is a '97 Cabernet Sauvignon from Napa Valley. A rare varietal. Two-seventy per bottle."

"That will do fine."

"And a glass for your guest?"

He shook his head no.

The waiter disappeared into the darkness.

It took a while for his eyes to adjust. Amid the charcoal stucco were various paintings—recreations of authentic Italian art—of naked people draped over other naked people. The walls were stenciled with vines and chrysanthemums. Fake shutters bordered the windows, painted to appear weathered. The open kitchen was full of entertainment as chefs in puffy hats tossed pans over open flames. Sizzling pans and banging pots interrupted the soft chatter of patrons.

He pulled a notebook and pen from the bag. On one of the pages he wrote: *Disregard my guest. Don't believe his lies. Pretend he doesn't exist.* He wrapped it inside a crisp hundred-dollar bill.

The waiter presented the wine and allowed him to smell the cork before pouring a glass.

"Your child-molester-looking friend has arrived. I will bring him to you now."

"Thank you, Anthony."

He extended his hand and the waiter accepted the handshake. A surprised expression filled the waiter's face as he stepped aside and read the note. The money vanished into his pocket.

"You are much too generous, sir."

While waiting for his guest, he dialed a pre-stored number on his cellular phone. It rang once.

"He just got here. I'll meet you at the van in thirty. I'll call again from outside."

"Have you heard of the Golden Rule?"

The waiter searched the ceiling for the answer. "If I am not mistaken, it is something along the lines of 'do to others as they have done to you.' Is that close, sir?"

"Do unto others as you would have them do unto you. Very good, Anthony. Honestly, I like your version better."

"Before I take your order," the waiters asked his guest, "would you like something to drink?"

"Shawn will be fine with water," he answered for him.

The waiter added a second menu to the table and left the two alone, never returning with water for his guest.

"How's it going, man?"

"Same shit, different day, Shawn." He could tell Shawn didn't recognize him as pulled a heavy object from the bag and placed it on the seat. "So, what's new with you, Shawny-boy? *My* wife is still doing her thing, kids growing up way too fast. But I'm hoping to tie up loose ends. You?"

It took him a while to respond.

"I'm getting married this summer," Shawn said.

"You and Milly?"

"No, *Wendy*. We're having an outside ceremony."

"You stopped seeing Milly after high school. I remember now. You were a senior and she was a freshman. Guess you legally *had* to stop seeing her, huh? Wendy was after that?"

"Not really. Wendy was a good while later, A few months ago. Before her there was Rebecca, and Erica, and then about a hundred others, it seemed, and then I found the perfect woman."

"Wendy McPherson. 1331 Feagleship road. Blonde hair. Hazel eyes. Five-foot-six. She goes by Becka sometimes?"

A long pause.

"You know her?"

"You could say that."

They both ordered some fancy pasta with chicken when Anthony returned. Once again, his guest asked for water, and once again his order went ignored.

He finished half the wine by himself, never once offering any to his guest, never once using his own name during conversation. They traded stories from when they were younger but they were never in the same story. And then he tested him, just to be sure.

"What's my name?"

"Huh?"

"You don't know my name, do you?"

Shawn was sweating over his food, avoiding eye contact.

"You have no idea who I am."

Shawn looked for the waiter.

"You *couldn't* know me. This is the first time we've met."

"What the hell *is* this?" Shawn said. "My secretary said I was having dinner with an old school friend. Who are you?" He stopped eating, his appetite suddenly gone. His fork clanked against the plate.

"Your secretary was misled. And you don't need to know who I am. It's irrelevant."

"I'm out of here."

Shawn threw his napkin on the table and stood.

"You're not going anywhere. Sit the fuck down." His voice never rose above a whisper.

"Look under the table."

"What?"

"Are you deaf? Look under the table."

His guest leaned down, lifted the table skirt. Waiting for him was the barrel of a Colt .38, pointed at his crotch.

"Oh, fuck me …" Shawn said, his voice trembling.

The hammer click was absorbed by the restaurant noise.

"If you do anything, I blow your balls off. Got it?"

Shawn nodded

"You're going to kill me. Jesus, you're really going to kill me." Shawn's face was soaked, his lips trembling.

"Calm down. Take a deep breath. I never said I was going to *kill* you. Do you know why you're here?"

"No."

"You're here because twelve years ago you raped a close friend of mine: Milly. You were eighteen; she was fourteen. We were just talking about her. You took her to the prom for sex. She pushed you away and you held her down and raped her."

"That was a long time ago, man."

"You will do everything I tell you, or you die. Understand?"

There was a sweat ring around his shirt collar and patches under his armpits.

The waiter waited by the bar until signaled.

"Say anything and I fucking kill you."

Shawn nodded, dripping onto the table.

Anthony scraped the last of the breadcrumbs.

"Can I get the two of you anything else?"

He handed the check to his new friend in the trench coat, who, in turn, after looking at the amount, passed it to his sweaty guest. The bill came to over four hundred dollars because of the wine.

He pushed the gun hard against Shawn's knee.

Shawn dug for his wallet and put a credit card in the plastic slot of the bi-fold.

"That will be all, thank you."

Anthony smiled and disappeared.

"What now?"

"After you finish paying for our meal, we go outside. You will walk casually to the exit and stop outside the door. If you run, I will shoot you in the back. I'll follow you out with the gun in my pocket. I can still shoot you through my pocket, so you don't want to try anything."

Anthony returned with the bill.

"Thank you. I hope you both have a wonderful evening."

"Wait," Shawn said.

A nudge under the table.

Shawn reluctantly took the receipt, sighed after realizing the amount, and signed his name. Above the scribble of signature, he tried to write some kind of distress note to the waiter. It was a good try.

As they walked by the registers, Anthony showed the receipt to his new friend in the trench coat.

Deciphering the word 'gun' made him smile as he led Shawn out of the restaurant, the .38 pointed to the rapist's back.

The air was cold and crisp outside. The moon, a smiling gray crescent, somehow found humor in all this. Their breaths displayed in white puffs, Shawn's a little more erratic.

He told him to wait by the curb and made a second call. A black van pulled into a vacant slot soon after and screeched to a stop. The van was windowless, besides those up front, which were tinted black.

He slid open the side.

"Get in."

The interior was furnished with horrid shag carpet and wood paneling. Metal rails were bolted to the vehicle's framework. A steel mesh screen separated the cab from the rest of the interior. A large Stanley deadbolt locked the rear doors from the inside.

He pushed him hard into the van and retrieved two sets of handcuffs from his duffle bag. With the gun in his face, Shawn didn't argue when he was told to handcuff himself to the railing with one set; the other required help. He positioned him so that he clung to the wall, his legs spread by a small crate.

Shawn craned his neck, shaking.

"What are you going to do to me?"

"Me? I'm not going to do anything."

He knocked against the metal screen.

"Through all this, you haven't even tried to apologize."

A beast of a man swiveled in the driver's seat. A knife scar sectioned his face. Three black tears tattooed below his eye.

"Remember the Golden Rule, Shawn? This is another friend of mine. His name is … well, it's not really important. He's been in prison for the last fifteen years. Last week he was released for good behavior."

The driver revealed a jack-o'-lantern smile.

"I think he wants a date for the prom."

FEAST OF CROWS

The crows land near
And dig us out
Their beaks pierce deep
To find cold blood

We dead can fear
But will not shout
Nor stir, nor weep
Through dirt and mud

Dead souls they eat
Each yearn the taste
Of death and rot
Too late to save

Dry bones, sick meat
Lost all but waste
A war is fought
At this old grave

EMPTY CANVAS

Her lifeless face centers the painting: milky white skin with royal purple lips and a set of dilated eyes with twin reflections of a hand holding a brush.

We crossed paths at a bakery and her smile was enough to imprison my need to put her on canvas. I learned from the man behind the counter that her name was Elle—quite a peculiar name, both memorable and tip-of-the-tongue. It rolls nicely out of the mouth to say such a name.

"Let me paint you," I said, catching up with her as she hailed for a taxi. She refused and so I tried again, a little less forward, but again she refused, waving off my charm. "I must capture your goddess figure," I pleaded, and then sank to my knees and begged like a child as she got in the cab. "I must paint you. I'll pay you for your time." Ultimately, she was unable to refuse and she let me slide in next to her on the seat.

It took a week to paint the body. She never slumped, her posture pristine—the perfect model. Elle held no objections to nudity as she displayed her vanity in my red Victorian chair. The knife through her chest offered freedom from such fear. She sat through the endeavor, her face always revealing that pious smile, her death keeping her motionless.

I painted her slender physique in a grayscale of sorts, using odd combinations of black and white. Her hair is black as pitch in the portrait, a wondrous waterfall covering half her face. Her skin is thus white with hints of ash, her lips—with that secret smile—a charcoal gray, eyebrows also black, of course, and many shades of mixed oils finishing the rest.

I managed to replicate her slightly sunken eyes and the carved features on her face. Her body, well, that is best left for the imagination; it would take pages of writing to provide an accurate description of such beauty.

Now that Elle is gone and buried, her role complete, I find myself staring hours on end at the portrait, transfixed on the eyes. They enrapture me. I look into those dilated pupils and see myself holding the paint brush. There are two in this painting.

THE MOST BEAUTIFUL PLACE

Shadows eclipse gray suns on white canvas
Escaping light is scarce
Revealed refractions of brightness dance
My heart thunders loudly
Wild flames spark in the darkness around
And in the center of it all I see myself

Surrounded am I by mountains and riverbed
Silken plains, soft pathways
Leading to more beautiful bends
My legs tremble with anxiety
In every direction a new journey awaits
And in the middle of it all I feel I am myself

At day's end a masterpiece is covered
A protection of compassion
With it comes great purpose
My body gains warmth
A comfort of pure completion, blanketed love
And under it all: you and me

UNSTITCHED LOVE

She saved his eyes for last—a glimpse of their emptiness before inverting the skin, filling his insides, and stitching together the gap between his legs. As if confused why Sally insisted on poking a needle through his hollow head, the incomplete stuffed bear twisted in her hands.

Aren't you finished with me yet?

Morning sunlight beamed through the blinds in parallel rays, dancing life onto its button eyes.

"Make me a teddy bear, make me another one, a better one," her sister insisted every few months.

How could Sally resist? Megan was only six—half Sally's age —and loved the little bears Sally crafted for her. Usually the stuffed creatures were small, no bigger than her hand; this one would stand over a foot tall.

"Make me a big one this time," Megan had said, "with droopy arms and floppy legs." Megan could be so demanding. "It has to have silver eyes, too."

It wasn't that Sally couldn't resist the chance to make another bear—it was because Sally was grounded for the weekend, thanks to Megan's tattling, and she had nothing better to do while caged in her bedroom.

Earlier that morning, Sally had stolen a brownish-green pair of Megan's holed jeans. After cutting the pant legs along their seams, Sally salvaged two ideal pieces of material. With a black felt pen, she drew the outline of a bear with droopy arms and floppy legs, and a round head with semicircle bumps for ears. There wasn't much body to the bear; he was mainly arms and legs connected to a head. Skinny appendages belled for hands and feet; all four met at the neck. Pleased with the design, she set the first pattern onto the second section of material, traced it with the pen, and cut out a nearly identical, two-dimensional figure.

Megan barged into the room. Sometimes Sally had to remind herself that Megan was only six. Still, she could be courteous and not scare her older sister half to death.

"Mom says not to use any more of my pants if you're making another bear."

"It's a little late now." Sally held the ruined jeans. "But they're your old pants, so Mom might not care."

"I'm still telling." Megan slammed the door behind her.

Stupid parents. Stupid sister. Stupid bear.

She tossed the two cutouts aside. One piece came to rest on a mess of toys and seemed to stand on its own.

Rummaging through her junk drawers, Sally found a spool of gray string and pulled a sewing needle from the kit she kept there. She retrieved the two bear halves and went back to work, sitting Indian-style on the floor. Upon completing the preliminary knot, where the legs connected, she sewed together the two flat pieces.

She had finished with the first leg and moved onto the side of the bear's head when Megan returned. Startled, Sally jabbed the needle into her hand, deep enough to draw blood.

"Don't you know how to knock, or at least open the door like a normal person?"

"You're in trouble." Megan stretched the four-syllable phrase.

"For what? What did *I* do?"

"You cut my pants. My *favorite* pair of pants."

"You never wear these anymore." She held the brown-ish-green remains. "That's why I chose this pair to begin with. You're such a snitch."

"*So ...*"

"That's exactly what I'm trying to do. I'm trying to *sew* your precious little bear, remember? And look, you made me bleed all over it."

A red splotch of blood had seeped into the material near the bear's neck. Sally turned it inside-out.

"At least it didn't go all the way through. It won't show. Go get me a Band-Aid, or I'll rip this precious bear in two."

Megan fled. At first, Sally thought she'd tattle, but she returned with a handful of bandages. Megan dropped them on the floor and left the room without another word. Sally fixed a Band-Aid to her palm, and set another aside for the bear.

By noon, she had finished sewing the bear's perimeter, all but the neck, from which she would turn the bear right-side-out. She studied the inline stitching that ran along the ragged material.

All this work for my brat of a sister.

She hated Megan, but loved her enough to finish the bear. The *last* bear. Sally was done pleasing her younger sister; from now on, Megan could make her own bears.

Sally opened Megan's dresser drawers and rummaged through them for a sweater. She found Megan's favorite, one with a chaotic silver pattern. It had shiny silver buttons that would suit beautifully as eyes. Sally ripped the third and sixth buttons free and shoved the sweater back into the dresser.

Sally stitched the buttons onto the bear, crisscrossing thread through the holes in their centers. She pricked her finger again as she fed the needle blindly through from the other side.

It took a while for the strange creature to look less spidery. She had left such a miniscule hole to feed the heavy material through. The arms and legs proved most difficult, but with the help of an unsharpened pencil, she was able to feed everything through the gap—head, buttons, all four appendages—and invert the bear. It was droopy and floppy. Megan would love it.

Her mother brought in a peanut butter and jelly sandwich and apple slices for lunch. She told Sally that a new pair of jeans for Megan would come out of her allowance.

"You can't go around cutting up good jeans whenever you feel like it," she had said. But Sally wasn't listening. She missed the concept behind the bears. They were toys Megan played with that, in the long run, no one would have to pay for since they were handmade.

Sally snuck downstairs and robbed a bag of dried beans from the kitchen. She funneled them into the ends of the bear's legs and then the arms. From her closet she pulled some bunting and filled the interior of the bear in a loose manner to keep it droopy and floppy. Sally sewed the magic portal shut and smiled.

She stitched pink thread in multi-parallel lines to help the half-circle ears stand out. Using a coarser black thread, she added thick "X" marks for a crooked smile, which made it appear as if the poor bear's lips had been stitched shut to keep him quiet.

Sally played with the bear—as much as any young girl could—and set it down, finally complete.

The bear could almost stand on its own accord. The bean-filled legs allowed it to stay in place with its head and arms hunched in an apelike stance. The bear kept falling forward whenever Sally tried to prop it upright.

Aren't you finished with me yet?

A tiny red flower of blood had seeped through the material after all, below the neck.

"Not done yet."

A smaller flower bloomed next to the first. The two red dots reminded Sally of old vampire movies. She picked up the Band-Aid she had set aside and covered the marks on the neck.

"Now you're finished."

She stabbed the sewing needle into the bear's sad face.

The bear stayed upright a moment before plopping to the ground, head tilted, mouth sewn shut, eyes lively from the early evening sun. Gray string, still looped through the needle, lay coiled at its heavy feet.

Drifting off to sleep, Sally thought of family, and not much else. She thought of Megan, who was ever so annoying, always whining and always tattling.

Make me this; make me that. Sally did this; Sally did that.

Sometimes Sally wished she could stitch that mouth shut with a spool of thread. She thought of her mom, who always punished, never listened, never cared and never gave hugs unless your name happened to be Meg, and thought of her dad, who was never there.

Sometimes she wished her parents dead.

A bright bulb of moon turned everything gray with shadows.

The bear was at the foot of Sally's bed, the needle and

string protruding from its cheek. Sally had deemed it a boy bear before going to bed. She named him Thatch, short for crosshatch, which she had always pronounced cross*thatch*. He faced the window, head tilted away from the rest of his body, smiling with his crooked, stitched mouth. Thatch's eyes reflected perfect circles of moon. A crow fluttered by the window, flickering light. For that moment, Thatch was alive.

At twelve past two in the morning, a scream startled Sally awake. It was Megan. The moon was gone. The room black. Sally could barely distinguish the silhouette of her sister sitting upright in bed. Megan shrieked a second time.

Mom and Dad racing down the hall.

Sally tried the lamp on the nightstand but knocked it over. It crashed onto the floor.

The bedroom door opened and Mom switched on the light. Megan screamed a third time.

"What's going on in here? Is everyone all right?"

Dad stood next to her, rubbing his eyes, trying to figure out why he was in his daughters' room at two-something in the morning.

"I broke my lamp, on accident, after Megan started screaming."

Megan cried, her chest bobbing.

Mom sat at her side and held her tight.

"Everything's okay now. You had a bad dream."

Megan was speechless.

"Sally, clean up that mess and get to bed, and be careful with the glass. Don't cut yourself."

Dad helped with the glass and went to bed.

"It wasn't a dream," Megan said through a face of tears. She pointed to the base of Sally's bed.

"The bear? Did the bear scare you?"

Sally leaned over, lifting the stuffed animal from the floor. "Thatch is just a stuffed animal, Meg. See, he's a dumb toy." She made him dance, the bear's arms and legs moving like a marionette without strings, the head slumped over, almost grinning.

"Stop it! Stop it!" her sister yelled, her face filling with tears.

"Put that thing away," Mom said. "Sally is teasing you."

Sally dropped it to the floor and it landed in a clump.

"It wasn't there before," Megan said, each word separated by a sob. "It was on my bed."

"I was asleep," Sally said, "until she started screaming, anyway. That's when I tried to turn on the light and knocked it over. Thatch was there all along … where I left him."

She pointed to the lump.

"Nuh-uh," said her sister. "I woke up and he was sitting on my stomach, staring. His eyes were glowing, and his neck was bleeding, and he had a needle sticking out of his head, and then …"

The rest was unintelligible.

"Put it away for the night," her mother said, swiping the bear from the floor. She gave it a quick inspection.

Megan yawned and rubbed her eyes. She was tucked into bed with a kiss on the forehead.

Mom took Thatch under an arm and poked herself with the needle. She swore under her breath, tossing the bear to the floor.

"You need to put things away when you're done with them," she whispered to Sally, who received no such goodnight kiss.

She shut off the light and kept the door ajar.

The room went dark, except for the wedge of light from the hall. A moment later, Sally heard the door to her parents' room close and the light disappeared, leaving the room dark.

Sally dreamt Thatch was alive. He sat on Megan's chest as she lay in bed, his silver button eyes reflecting her terrified, hopeless expression. The needle stuck out of his face, gray string dangling. Thatch's droopy arms played within the scarlet jelly around Megan's neck. Scissors skewered her shoulder.

Megan reached a weakened, blood-streaked arm to her sister. Two fingers and a thumb curled upward, gesturing for help while her skinny wrist shook. Her pinky and ring fingers stayed behind on the pillow. Megan pleaded, but she only produced a strained, choking gibberish.

Sally cried out, but no footsteps raced through the hall, which meant Thatch had gotten to their parents first.

The bear's head slowly pivoted. The bear she had crafted using pants and buttons and whatnot. The bear she had named Thatch. The bear she had brought to life. As his head turned to face her, Sally noticed the Band-Aid on his neck was gone. Two holes of red were in its place, oozing blood.

It was Sally's blood in the bear, Sally giving him life. Glowing eyes hypnotized her, and she wanted to scream. But her sister wasn't screaming, not anymore. Megan was dead, like Mom and Dad. Sally's family was gone.

It was then she noticed Thatch didn't have a mouth. The silver eyes were there, and the pink ears, but the thick stitching of his mouth was gone. Holes remained where thread had crisscrossed in a crooked smile. On his face was a connect-the-dots constellation of grin. Thatch held Sally in a frozen scream.

She woke in a blanket of sweat, her heart racing, her entire body shaking. She buried herself in the covers and made sure to tuck her feet and hands underneath. Covered, she was safe.

Eventually the bed became an oven. Body heat filled her makeshift safety blanket. Thatch was out there in the darkness, ready to pounce at the first glimpse of exposed flesh. She'd poke out her toe, and he'd grab it and pull out the rest of her.

But it was only a dream. Megan was alive. So were her parents.

Clenching her teeth, she poked out a toe, ready to feel a soft jean hand wrap around it. A breeze greeted the toe, and nothing more. She slipped the rest of the foot out, and then the other. Her fingers crawled out next; one by one they curled the edges of the comforter and found the cold bedroom air. Sally pulled her head free but kept her eyes sealed.

It was only a bad dream.

She had to check the base of her bed. Thatch would be there for sure, plopped onto his side and staring stupidly at nothing. She opened her eyes and leaned over the edge.

Thatch lay flat against the floor, his appendages sprawled like the compass on a map. One arm pointed to Megan, the other to Sally; one leg pointed to the door, the other to the window.

This was all Megan's fault: the nightmare, the paranoia.

Sally headed to the dresser where she kept her craft supplies and pulled out a pair of scissors. Moonlight shimmered on the sharp blades. Sally's smile widened as she ventured to the edge of her bed.

She sat next to Thatch and propped him up to face her. He

did nothing to stop her, his head tilted to the side. She stabbed the scissors into his neck until they tore through. From the wound, she pulled at the stuffing. Everything had to come out. She pulled and pulled. She'd save the eyes for last—those silver lifeless discs. She'd rip them out.

The creature bled.

Red erupted from the wound.

But isn't this my blood?

Thatch remained lifeless as Sally tore out his insides. Still he bled, and soon she sat in sticky red.

She held out her hands; they were covered..

I'm dreaming.

Sally checked her fingers, her palms, her wrists. Nowhere could she find a cut. It wasn't her blood. She grabbed the creature's paw, clipped off the tip. More blood poured out.

I must be dreaming.

The creature bore those shiny eyes into hers as it struggled to break free. Sally held it down as she let it bleed out. It writhed, and squirmed, and would speak to Sally if not for the stitching that sealed its mouth.

Wake up!

She waited for her parents. For once, she wanted to hear their footsteps down the hall. She wanted to see her sister.

Wake up!

Snapping out of it, Sally sat upright and shuttered, sobbing aloud to no one. The house was dead. Megan lay beneath her in a pool of blood. Scissor handles protruded from her neck. The tips of a few fingers were scattered on the pillow. Megan wore a Band-Aid with two red dots underneath. Her mouth, stitched shut in crisscrosses of thick black thread, smiled wanly; cobwebs of bunting poked from the gaps. Her head was tilted at a curious angle. And those eyes …

WAR

Rapture and bloodshed and grievance and death
(things we endure)
Fold in the walls of our minds and our flesh
Charred skin, blackened souls, a baby's last breath
Spill in the streets of our homes as we thresh
(things we ensure)

Torture and hatred and famine and blame
(things so impure)
Hold in the gall of our hearts as we find
Marred sin, slackened goals, a father's last shame
Shrill in the feats of our cold and our bind
(things so secure)

THE GIRL IN THE RED FLOWER PATTERN DRESS

A girl in a white flower pattern dress ran in front of us and I opened her chest and neck with a single squeeze of the trigger as three quick-shots *chut-tut-tut* tore her up in a red arc that blossomed from her chest. I nudged her with my boot but she was lifeless, her eyes glossy and as confused as my own. Her thin arms held an assault rifle, her fingers nowhere near the trigger. Her dead hands grabbed the stock as if she were going to stab one of us with the barrel. It's rumored some of the people we were fighting believed they could make bullets leave the guns faster if they pressed harder and faster against the trigger. The people we were fighting. The people we were protecting. The little girl in the dress wasn't a day over ten. She looked just like my daughter Lacy, her soft tan skin smooth and innocent. I remember her dead face.

We formed a diamond and I was the lead. Taylor was already dead, so that left four of us in the squad. Knots was my left wing and Anderson my right. Pips played clean-up at the tail. In this formation, we were nearly unstoppable. Pips and I were the closest. We went through boot camp together. Everyone in camp called him Pips, short for Henry L. Pipson. Everyone had nicknames. Knots was really James T. Smith. We called him Knots because he was good with rope. One night at base camp we tied him to the bed after he fell asleep. We laughed our asses off the next morning. Anderson was simply 'Anderson' because we felt sorry for him for having such a pansy name: Marion Wetherbury Anderson, III; that, and because the man was built like a gorilla. He had more muscle on his body than our squad combined. They called me Jap, short for Jason A. Parker. I was either Jap, or *The* Jap, depending on the conversation.

I sent my little girl that same joke in my last letter back home. Lacy sometimes pressed the tips of her fingers to the corners of her eyes and sang that little jingle: "Chinese, Japanese, In-between," as she moved her eyelids in different slants. Cutest little thing, my daughter, but man, we could be such racist fucks back home. My ex would never talk to me again if she ever found out I taught her that. She probably still thinks I dumped Lacy in her lap and fled, but that wasn't the case. I didn't have a choice, getting laid off and all. I was tired of searching for employment for months on end, sucking Welfare's teat until the checks stopped arriving in the mail. I finally had enough restless nights. My girl deserved something better. Serve my time, get paid, go home; that was the plan. As I looked over the dead girl in the street, I thought of Lacy. I thought of some poor Iraqi soldier going to war in America, mowing down my little girl in the street where she grew up. How would her father feel? How would *I* feel?

The four of us approached a building pock-marked with bullet holes, and the same color as the sand at our feet. A cloth sign was strung to the side of the entrance door which read: AMERICA AIDS IS FUCK. An upside-down American flag draped over the canopy, a broad, red-brown splash of blood crossing out the front of it.

As I watched my desecrated flag flap in the hot sun, a gunshot brought a body to the ground. Anderson had seen him before any of us: a young man perched on the rooftop. He fell from the clay shingles and landed hard on the ground. If the single round hadn't killed him, his neck had snapped from the fall, an awful sound.

We were four sets of eyes and four sets of ears as we moved in formation. I remember the dog tags of Taylor Nighey jangling in my pocket, reminding me of his death earlier that morning. After tripping a Bouncing Betty, the shrapnel within converted his body to Swiss cheese. If he had been with us at the AMERICA AIDS IS FUCK house, things may have turned out differently. It should have been a routine sweep. Nothing special. I held the MK-5 tight to my chest, shoulder-level, as I freed a magnesium grenade dangling from my uniform. Pips had his pistol ready, his choice for close combat. My eyes moved to Knots, who shouldered his own MK-5. Anderson switched to the SAW, an appropriately named weapon considering we were slaughtering our competition. Before Nighey died, we were quick, efficient; we were a lot of things past tense.

The flash bang did the hard work. I threw it through a broken window and the snap of it sent the room in disarray. Voices rose from the silence, full of fear and confusion. Several gunshots went off inside, and I imagined men holding hands in front of their faces as they shot at the white that blinded them. Shouts led to more gunshots and finally the first of many stormed out the door. I took the first one out with another three quick-shots. It usually worked this way. There would be one, and then a quick succession of two or three more. This would be followed by us entering the building and clearing it of all discernable life. Men, women, children; if they posed a threat, the threat was eliminated.

Anderson moved in with the SAW. Five or six people spilled out of the room. The SAW turned them into hamburger meat with a quick *braaaaaaaaaaaat!* before I could yell at Knots to secure the door. I trailed behind Knots while Pips held our backs safe from the street.

We spread and reformed our diamond, this time Anderson leading with me and Knots to either side. We shifted easily in this manner, often moving like a Ouija board planchette. The remaining men in the first room were heavily disoriented. I shot one as he dove for a bolt-action rifle on the floor. Another *braaaaaaaaaaaat!* of Anderson's SAW shredded the room to confetti. Knots fired a dozen rounds on auto-fire and dropped two more. Pips was behind me popping rounds in the chaos. I lost sight of him for a moment, which I shouldn't have, but watched him put a bullet above the eyes of another that entered from an adjacent room. And then the riot calmed. Anderson held up a hand for cease fire.

I was about to relay our next maneuver when something metal bounced across the floor. Through the falling confetti and dust clouds and gore, we barely noticed the grenade. The four of us looked to the sound, Knots to his feet. It erupted under him and sent the upper half of his body to the ceiling and the lower half of his body to oblivion. Anderson was thrown against a wall more than ten feet away. From the ground, he switched to his pistol and shot an old woman, but not before she put a bullet in Anderson's shoulder and another in his neck. Red spewed from the hole as Anderson covered the wound and shot her four times. Both fell to the floor.

Within seconds, Knots was dead and so was Anderson.

Pips looked to me and I looked to Pips and Pips grabbed his own grenade from his chest, pulled the pin, and threw it through the door. The explosion was twice that of the hostile's grenade and soon *our* room showered us with what previously filled *their* room. Pieces of furniture and glass and torsos and papers and legs and everything else erupted from the door. Not until after the five of us became four and the four of us became two and we remaining two finished clearing the building did I notice the triangle-shaped piece of vase sticking out from Pips' abdomen. At first he didn't notice it but then I noticed it and he saw me notice and his eyes went wide at the blood and then he asked me, "Do I pull it out or leave it in? Oh God oh fuck, oh God, Jap, what do I do?"

I was about to tell him to leave it in, but he reached down and sliced his hands and pulled it loose and blood poured out of him to the floor and he tried to hold it in but it didn't matter because some old towel-head bastard came out of nowhere and put a bullet through Pip's face, below his left eye, and I saw him blink red once as his skull burst out the back.

I made eye contact with the man who shot him. His weathered hands shook as if he had never shot nor held a gun before in his life. His other hand held a young girl behind him as he shielded her and moved the gun to me. My MK-5 clicked when I pulled the trigger. I was going to kill them both, unsure what else to do. My brothers were dead. His family was dead, all but his little girl, who could have been the twin of the one I ripped apart in the street moments before my squad stormed into their home. Before the grenade blew Knots into a thousand pieces. Before Anderson was shot through the neck and bled to death. Before this dumb fuck blasted out the back of Pip's head.

"Look what you did," I told him, pointing to the mess.

He said something in his language and then in English he said, "America," as if cursing the word, the gun shaking in his hand. The gun pointing at me. He could barely hold the thing. Tears ran along his dirty cheeks. His daughter, I could only guess, peeked out from around him. She was crying and wore a white flower pattern dress like her sister outside. They could be twins, no older than ten. No older than Lacy.

"Put the gun down," I told him, but I wasn't in the position to negotiate.

The room was quiet but it rang in my ears. It smelled of smoke and clay and sulfur and death and I took all of it in: a wooden chair burning behind a charred desk in the corner; a cracked family portrait, crooked on the wall and burning; a stroller knocked onto its side, the doll strapped into it missing an eye, its black melted face smiling at me; one of Knots' boots and part of his foot still inside.

"We're here to help you." I could barely hear my own voice, nor could I believe it.

He said something and the gun lowered.

I took a slow step forward, leaned down, set my automatic rifle on the ground, and lifted my hands into the air.

The little girl pointed to the door and screamed, "Annalah!" as she saw her sister in the street for the first time.

From my position, I could see the dead girl's shoes and part of her dress soaking the blood, but nothing more. Three quick-shots *chut-tut-tut* had ripped her open, a girl no older than my daughter.

He tried holding the girl, but she slipped away and I took the chance and rushed him with the knife from my belt and slid it into his neck, to the hilt, moved it downward into his throat.

I tasted his coppery breath as he gargled something incoherent and squeezed the trigger.

We wrestled to the floor, his hand around my neck, my hand pushing hard into his face, his other hand holding the gun against the hole in my thigh and my other hand twisting the handle of the knife into his neck. As we both lay on the cold floor in this odd embrace, he looked to me with those dead eyes and said something I couldn't understand with lips that didn't make sense, nor sound, like some kind of fish trying to breathe out of water, this desert man in the sand out in the sun without any water, and I watched as the life drained out of him as he tried to tell me something I could never understand.

I thought about life and about death and peace and war as I crawled. I left behind a trail of blood across the cluttered floor. I dragged my body to Pips first because he was closest. His eyes were open, so I shut them and yanked the tags from his collar. I found the upper half of Knots and took his tags. Anderson was next to him, so I grabbed those as well. I'm not sure why I took their tags. Someone would have followed behind us to play clean-up, to assess the situation, to claim the dead. Someone always did. No man left behind, or some shit. They were my brothers and it felt right taking all of them with me.

The little girls that resembled Lacy were outside and I crawled over to them. The one still alive held the one I shot and rocked her gently, singing something sweet into her ear that sounded like an Iraqi lullaby. Both sets of eyes were open and lifeless. I remember the little girl running in front of us. The assault rifle in her arms nothing more than a piece of wood carved to resemble a weapon. Her fingers nowhere near the trigger. I remember their frozen faces as the white dresses soaked the red.

BLACK

How can we see there is love in the world
When you blind us with darkness?
Behind this darkness waits death,
And lies,
In a red-swirled mess of blood,
This hurricane of deceit,
This mud.
It's you:
Your cries,
Your breath.
You look down from your high seat.
It's you.

You wear black in this sick game you call life.
You wear black in this black-and-white world.
You wear black.
You wear black.

How can we see there is love in the world
When you hide us in shadow?
Behind this shadow is hate,
And war,
Where we are called to choose sides,
These conflicts of religion,
These tides.
It's you:
Your core,
Your fate.
You look down with conviction.
It's you.

You wear black in this sick game you call life.
You wear black in this black-and-white world.
You wear black.
You wear black.

BRICK HOUSE

She ran her tongue across my teeth and at first I didn't know what to do, but then my body told me to open my mouth and to taste the mint on her breath and to feel the wet warmth she offered me. Her smile got me to smile.

I wasn't sure I wanted Erica Lock so close to my face, but that is how we ended up, inches away from one another. I remember smelling spearmint and blushing as she placed her hand on the back of my neck. Her amber eyes bounced right to left and left to right while I tried to keep up with them. She traced the edges of my lips with her scarlet fingernails and I trembled. I brought my own hand to her cheek and connected her freckles with an imaginary line, feeling the single dimple at the corner of her mouth, the cat scratch scar on her chin, the soft skin of her neck and the pulse of our two hearts beating rhythmically together.

It was a strange mix of fear and confusion as these emotions crashed oddly together as one: love. Did I love her? We had only just met the summer before our sophomore year of college. Did I want her inches from my face? Did I want her looking into my eyes so lustfully? Did I want her to trace my lips with her fingers, to grab my neck, to lean into me with her body pressed ever so gently against my own? I wasn't sure at the time, but it felt right somehow as she ran her tongue across my teeth, melting me deep into her arms as she wrapped them around me.

I closed my eyes, knowing she was still watching them to see what I would do, and then I leaned into her and opened my mouth slightly and let her in and tasted the mint as she fed it to me. Her hand got lost deep in my hair as blood rushed upward from my chest and downward to the rest of my body—losing my breath and losing my mind—and I could not breathe as she sucked the air from my lungs, and I could not breathe as my heart palpitated, and I could not breathe as she pulled away and took my heart.

Finally I opened my eyes to see Erica Lock, her eyes no longer dancing. She trembled and I could feel her heart beating through her chest and through her breasts because they were pressed against me. She took in air between trembling lips. I touched them with the tip of a finger, moving to the dimple at the edge of her smile. My other hand held the small of her back and I could feel the dampness of sweat. I remember feeling her hand in my hair and I wanted it to stay there forever. I didn't want the moment to end although moments before I was unsure I even wanted it to begin.

And then my mother walked in on us.

It was an unexpected visit, to say the least. She wanted to see my dorm, to make sure I was doing fine on my own, to make sure I was eating healthy and keeping my room clean, to see if I was living to the hype I relived to her through e-mail. She didn't want to walk in on me holding a girl. She didn't want to see us kissing, but that didn't matter. I didn't date much in high school. I didn't go to Homecoming, Sade Hawkins, Prom, or any other dance. She didn't want me to date until I turned sixteen and after I turned sixteen I honestly wasn't ready to date. I was still searching for myself, and until I could find myself, I wasn't sure

I wanted to share it with anyone.

She caught me masturbating once. I forgot to lock the door and was naked on my back, the bed sheet crumpled at my legs. It must have slid down while I was finding myself. I was in mid-orgasm when the door opened, my back arched into the air. The expression on her face changed from innocent to horror-stricken as my face changed from coital to horrorstricken. I pulled the sheets over my body and yelled at her to get out as the spasms between my legs lessened and my heartbeats hastened. She gasped and slammed the door. I gasped trying to catch my breath as I tried to rejoin my mind with my body and tried to forget my stupidity for not locking the door.

Twice she had walked in on me unexpectedly. Twice she had found me gasping for air at my most intimate of moments.

"Get your hands off my daughter," my mother said when she saw us on the bed in my dorm room.

Erica took her advice and took a lock of my hair with it; somehow, while caressing my neck, she had gotten some of my ponytail stuck in her ring.

This is the part of the story where some of you will be taken aback; flipping to reread the last few pages to make sure you didn't miss anything. Some sort of trick, perhaps. The only trick is that some of you assumed I was male and are now shocked to find me otherwise. Some of you will even stop reading and set this story aside, disgusted. Whether or not you accept it, the truth about me is simple: I have a second X chromosome; I have a vagina. There is no gimmick. Love is love. This is a love story. This is a tragedy. This is a story about two people becoming one and I don't expect you to like it. In fact, I don't want you to like it; I want you to hate it. I want you to feel saddened by the time you reach the end.

The young woman at my side hid her face and I tried to pull her hand away, but she turned to the window. My mother pointed at her and said, "I won't have you turn my daughter into no *lesbian*." She said the word like a curse, like it was a bad thing for one woman to love another.

"Mom! Get out!"

But she stayed. She sized me from head to toe, disgusted, her upper lip curled. I had tainted the holy body she had given me by "experimenting" as she put it. I tried telling her I wasn't experimenting with anything. I was finding myself. I was finding love. I was finding a way to express the feelings deep in my body that wanted out. They wanted Erica Lock.

"Tess," she sighed, and that was all she wanted to say by the tone in her voice—my name—but then she said something that would make me hate her for the next few years.

Four simple words: *you're not my daughter.*

"What?" Both Erica and I said it at the same time. Erica faced me and then glared at my mother. I truly fell in love with her then. Clammy hands bound us together as she scooted closer. I think it was then, as well, that Erica fell for me.

"You're not my daughter," my mother repeated.

A single tear fell from my eye and ran along the bridge of my nose. I felt it drip and land on my blouse.

"Because of this?"

Erica looked at our hands.

"You don't love her," my mother said. "You don't understand love. I always knew there was something wrong with you. Your father and I both thought you might find out someday, but this, this fad, this phase, this whatever it is in your life, it should prove to you that you're not my daughter—" She cut herself short and wouldn't even look at us.

We disgusted her.

"But Dad—"

"Your father is dead, Tess. He and your mother died after you were born. We didn't want to tell you because we thought you'd do something drastic, like this …"

I wanted to kiss Erica in front of her. I wanted to disgust her, then, by reaching my hands under Erica's shirt, pulling her shirt over her head and pulling her toward me as our mouths connected. But that would be unfair to Erica and that's not what I wanted to do. I wanted to slap my … *this woman* across the face for belittling me, for disowning me so easily because of fear.

"And Katie?"

"I gave birth to your sister, just not you. James, your adoptive father …" She kept rambling, but I stopped listening.

James had been my father for twenty years of my life; my mother … *not my mother*, she made him a stranger in a moment; she had made herself a stranger. Because I kissed a girl, because she walked in on me while I was finding myself—twice now— and because I no longer fit within her daughter mold, she had disowned me. Part of me didn't want to believe her.

I rose from the bed. She took half a step back because I was nothing but a sick little girl to her.

"Look at me," I said, and it took her a while, but she finally did. "I fucking hate you." I said it just above a whisper. I made sure she was looking into my eyes so she knew I meant every word.

Tears ran freely from my eyes. She was letting me go and I was letting her go. I let her slap me across the face and when she left I locked the door.

During Katie's sixteenth birthday party, I had an odd conversation with her about boys. Katie wasn't supposed to start dating until she turned sixteen, but she had been seeing this boy named Zach since she was fifteen. When we were alone, Katie asked me what sex was like and I told her sex was like electricity riding up your spine. She admitted to having sex once, but it was nothing like electricity, and that it hurt. I explained to her that it would eventually stop hurting and that she'd probably become addicted to it.

"Mom won't go with me to get birth control."

I asked if she and Zach had used a condom and she said Zach had a million of them in his sock drawer, but for the most part what they did together didn't call for protection.

"When did *you* start having sex?" she asked me.

My first time was in Junior year of high school. Some jock named Joss Thompson. She asked if it hurt and I said yes, at first. She asked if it felt like electricity riding up my spine. It didn't. It felt like a five minute violation of my body, but I didn't tell Katie that. I told her what she needed to be told, that love is an emotion, and without love, sex is just two people fucking.

We laughed and then Mom and Dad walked around the corner and surprised us.

"What's so funny?"

Katie told them we were discussing boys.

"Boys, huh?" Mom said.

Katie didn't know about my relationship with Erica.

Dad pretended someone flagged him down and left the three of us alone. Outside, a mixture of adolescent boys and girls were throwing water balloons at one another.

"You tell Katie you're seeing someone?"

Katie let out a high-pitched noise and punched me.

"What's his name—do I know him—is he cute?"

"*Mom* ..."

"Your sister's *dying* to know, Tess. Look, she's ecstatic."

She was. Her eyes were glossy from the florescent lighting in the kitchen.

"Electricity," she said and giggled.

"Fine," I finally said. "Lock."

Katie grabbed my arm and said, "Is there emotion, or are you two just, you know ..."

I did know, but Mom didn't, so I told her.

"Yes, there is love."

My mother rolled her eyes and folded her arms. "Lock's just the last name," she said. "Why don't you tell Katie the rest of *his* name."

I smiled at my little sister, hesitated, and then came out of my imaginary closet.

"Erica Lock."

The corner of my mother's lips curled again.

Katie gave a crooked smile and said, "Erica Lock? But that's my friend Jennifer's older sister—oh." There was shock in her voice, but no disgust. "So you're ... and she's ..."

I nodded and she asked the question I expected her to ask.

"And there's emotion, and electricity?"

"It's like Nikola Tesla put a Jacob's ladder between my legs."

My mother stormed away and joined the party outside.

My sister was the first person I ever told.

"Cool," she said. "Does my friend Jennifer know about her sister? I won't say anything."

She knew.

And then Katie asked me questions about sex and boys and semen and we walked outside to have some fun on her birthday.

Erica and I stayed together until our senior year of college. I met her parents once. I was introduced to them as one of her girlfriends from school and they just assumed I was just another one of her friends. If we were both boys and I was instead introduced as one of her boyfriends, they may have thought of us differently.

Our relationship was hidden. We'd hang out between classes, share lunches, go to the movies on the weekends and out to dinner, but we never shared anything physical with the public. Every once in a while we'd get to talking and one of us would brush the other's hand, but we usually caught ourselves. Sometimes, at the theatre, after the lights dimmed, we'd hold hands, but only if we were alone in the row. Sometimes it was difficult to hide our emotions. Our emotions weren't socially accepted.

One day Erica and I sat alone under the elm tree outside the chemistry building finishing homework assignments when she said, "Let's do it."

I remember looking up from my calculus book and saying, "I can't. I have volleyball practice in an hour and a monster history test tomorrow morning."

"No, not *it* it. Let's come out. Why should we hide the fact that we love each other?"

Butterflies fluttered in my stomach, as if I were going to float away. I was in love with Erica Lock, but had never told her, and it was the first time I heard her say that she loved me.

I looked around to see if anyone were watching—part of me didn't care—before grabbing her hand within my own.

"Do you want to?"

I told her I did and then I leaned forward to kiss her.

Before our lips could make contact, jock Bobby Allison and his friend Trey walked by and Bobby said, "Trey, check it out."

A finger pointed in our direction.

"Nice ..." said Trey.

"Sick," said Bobby, but 'sick' had recently become synonymous for 'bitchin,' the same way 'bad' had changed meaning in the mid-eighties from something bad to something good.

"Yeah," said Trey, "lesbians are so fucking hot."

And then they were gone. Erica laughed and I laughed and we were both blushing because we were both out now, and with Bobby and Trey seeing what they saw, rumors of us having wild sex in public under the elm tree by the chemistry building would soon spread.

The rumors indeed spread and soon it seemed as if the entire campus knew about us. People were constantly turning their heads. At the time, there were a few outed individuals and only one other couple, but as the weeks turned to months, more and more students came out—to us, anyway.

"I wish I had the nerve to come out," said a boy from my calculus class, and then, "You won't tell anyone, will you? It's just between us?"

One girl from track came up to me one day and said, "If you ever need anyone to talk to ..." and then she walked away.

If I could put a number to it, I would say about a tenth of all the people I knew at school were gay, teachers included. I quickly learned their secrets.

Things were good until the Saturday before our graduation. We were on our way to get some iced coffees when Erica said, "Isn't that your mom?"

It was. She was walking out of a small bookstore called Hidden Passages. She held a book, but I couldn't make out the title because her purse was pressed against the cover as she dug for money.

"You want to go somewhere else?"

Something inside me said we should try someplace else, but I was tired of hiding from my mother.

We followed her inside and once we were in line I said casually, "Hey, Mom," as if we had just seen each other not too long ago. It had been close to six months since we last spoke, and it wasn't on good terms.

"Hey, sweetie," she said before giving me a hug.

I still couldn't read the title of the book. I had no idea why she felt the impulse to hug me, but it felt nice to feel that connection with her again.

"Erica, right?"

She gave Erica a hug, too. Well, half a hug. This wasn't my mother. I was surprised she even remembered her name.

"Can I buy the two of you some coffee?"

Erica and I shared confused expressions and we both half-smiled. Who was this woman?

"Sure," I said, and then the three of us were ordering.

When she paid the cashier, she set the book on the counter and I read the binding: *My Girl Likes Girls*, or something similar. I can't quite remember the exact title because of the events that happened next, but it was something close to that and it was the first time my mother ever tried understanding me. The book was a start, at least. It was cute.

We got our drinks after waiting through an uneasy silence and my mother asked if we wanted to sit together at one of the tables outside. As we walked out the door, a noisy diesel truck roared down the street. It belonged to one of the aggies that went to our college. I can still remember his face, but not his name, as if it were erased from my mind. There was another in the cabin and three others crouched in the truck bed.

I still remember the hatred behind one of their voices, which yelled, "Goddamn dikes!" as the rusted truck raced by us.

The brick hit Erica across the bridge of her nose, diagonally from her eye to her cheekbone, and I will never forget the sound it made striking her. She fell immediately and I grabbed her hand and fell with her. She landed hard on the sidewalk, cracking the back of her head.

My mother dropped her book and dropped her coffee and hid her own nose with her hands and stared at the mess they had made of Erica Lock. Blood welled at the gash across her face and at the back of her head. What was left of the brick lay scattered around her body in a half dozen broken pieces.

Erica still held onto her coffee cup as her eyes rolled into her head and she convulsed.

"Oh my God!" my mother screamed.

I grabbed the back of Erica's head and placed a hand across the wound and felt pieces of cheekbone shift under my fingertips as I tried to hold in the red that so eagerly wanted out of her. She sputtered as she tried to talk but after a moment she was silent. She stopped breathing. Her pulse slowed and soon I could no longer feel it beating against my skin.

My mother was silent. God wouldn't take her away from the horror. The book she had purchased to help her understand me lay open, the life of my love pooling around it and soaking into its pages. She knelt next to me and removed her scarf and held it against Erica's head as she screamed for someone to call an ambulance while tears rolled down her face. She tried to hold

Erica together while I performed CPR.

I switched from compressions to respirations, wondering what my mother thought of me as I put my lips to Erica's so she could breathe me in. It was the first time I kissed her in public—in front of my mother, in front of anyone—but no one seemed to mind. She tasted like spearmint and all I could think about was our first kiss, with our faces inches from one another, the trembling, our pulses beating together rhythmically, and then Erica opened her eyes and gasped for air, her back arching slightly.

One of her eyes was swollen shut, but the other bounced right to left and left to right as I tried to keep up with it. She reached with a shaky hand and traced my lips and then ran her fingers through my hair. Through all of her confusion and pain I could make out the beginning of a dimple at the corner of her mouth when she tried to smile. As her hand fell to her side I noticed some of my hair was stuck in her ring.

She closed her eyes and died.

THE BETRAYER

This glass is not a glass
But a mirror through which I see
That everything inside is me
Those red eyes are not eyes
But a reflection of curiosity
That burn this apprehended me
This fake me
This me who is not me
This negativity

He walks inside my shoes
Those black shoes of rot
That house this man I'm not
He speaks with twisted tongue
Beneath a wretched voice I ought
To recognize but fought …
This new me
This me who is not me
This divinity

This demon reaches out
And passes through the mirror
My eyes they never tear
Those red eyes are not my eyes
But a reflection of my fear
Which snatch my soul unclear
This is me
This me who is not me
This reality

THE TRIAL CHAIR

The Original Hippocratic Oath:

I swear by Apollo, Asclepius, Hygieia, and Panacea, and I take to witness all the gods, all the goddesses, to keep according to my ability and my judgment, the following Oath. To consider dear to me, as my parents, him who taught me this art; to live in common with him and, if necessary, to share my goods with him; to look upon his children as my own brothers, to teach them this art. I will prescribe regimens for the good of my patients according to my ability and my judgment and never do harm to anyone. To please no one will I prescribe a deadly drug nor give advice which may cause his death. Nor will I give a woman a pessary to procure abortion. But I will preserve the purity of my life and my arts. I will not cut for stone, even for patients in whom the disease is manifest; I will leave this operation to be performed by practitioners, specialists in this art. In every house where I come I will enter only for the good of my patients, keeping myself far from all intentional ill-doing and all seduction and especially from the pleasures of love with women or with men, be they free or slaves. All that may come to my knowledge in the exercise of my profession or in daily commerce with men, which ought not to be spread abroad, I will keep secret and will never reveal. If I keep this oath faithfully, may I enjoy my life and practice my art, respected by all men and in all times; but if I swerve from it or violate it, may the reverse be my lot.

1

"Just another damned short story about rapture." It was the last thing Charles Pierce said to his wife before he threw the pages into the trash and left the house. He was nearly finished with the first draft—ten thousand measly words, but at least it was something. It was difficult to find time to write with the bills and the job and the wife and their son and daughter's constant racket as they ran around the house and mocked the sounds coming from the television. He had tuned them all out, the words starting to flow from the old typewriter, the perfect ending ready to leap from his mind and onto the page. Rachel chimed in at that defining moment of closure, those last few keywords that would tie everything together. It was right there waiting for him … "What are you working on, honey?" she had asked, and the words just disappeared.

He slammed the door and heard the picture frame on the wall crash to the floor, the glass within its wooden frame shattering. It was a picture of the four of them, Charles remembered, as the gravel driveway crunched beneath his feet. They were crouched near a fountain from some water park. Rachel liked the photo. It was one of the few pictures of them together, smiling and happy.

"What am I working on? What kind of a fucking question is that? I'm working on a short story about rapture, about ecstasy, about finding joy in torturing others. That's what I'm working on." He was talking to himself again, but that didn't matter. Sometimes it felt right talking to himself. "Who needs a therapist? I'm my own personal therapist."

He regretted throwing the story away. It was a good story. He would later have to dig it out of the trash for revisions.

The antagonist was much like Charles: dark, demeaning, and enigmatic. He didn't have a name yet, so in the manuscript he's referred to as The Stranger, a horrible thing to call a character, but would work until a proper name filled its place. The main character was a poor fellow named Robert Shrub, a play on the name Robert Plant. Basically, it was a survival story. Rachel would hate it. She didn't care much for violence.

"Lucidity," provisionally titled, was loaded with excess violence and started with action, something he rarely did with his fiction. It reminded him of Douglas E. Winter's novel, *Run*, with the pressure building and building and never letting up, the constant run-on sentences that somehow worked to create fluidity and a sense of speed. His protagonist, Rob, wakes to the whine of a power drill, discovering he's flat on his back, naked, and crucified to a cross with rope binding him in place. The Stranger wears a white papier-mâché mask to cover his face, but the mask looks like Rob. There are no eyelets, no nostril holes, no sliver of mouth from which to breathe, just a solid featureless face of white. He holds the drill for Rob to see before squeezing the trigger and pressing the bit into the wood until the scent of burnt pine joins them in the otherwise empty room. He rests the tip against Rob's thigh. The eighth-inch bit burns against his bare skin. The trigger is squeezed once again and the bit passes through his leg until the coppery scent of blood replaces the pine. It sticks deep into bone as the clutch on the drill grates. Instead of reversing the bit free, The Stranger snaps it off and leaves it protruding from his leg like some kind of slipshod acupuncture.

All of this is in the first paragraph.

Charles opened the door to the Civic and hopped inside. He sat there a while, put the key in, turned it enough to play the stereo. A Led Zeppelin song was fading out with Jimmy Paige on the guitar. He couldn't help but smile. The next song wasn't worth the radio play so he turned the key the rest of the way, started the car, and drove out of town.

It wasn't the first time he'd driven away from Rachel. He'd make a U-turn just before the bridge; that would give him fifteen minutes there, fifteen back. He needed to clear his head and half an hour of alone time would do just fine. Charles thought about the pages sitting in the trash, thought of what waited for him in the glove compartment, and then focused on the road.

2

It burns his throat like swallowing lava. The more he drinks, the more he forgets. A quarter of the bottle is gone. Charles pours himself another glass and tries to focus through the vodka to a wavy image of the water trickling under the bridge. The summer has taken most of the creek away, but it runs. He holds the glass tumbler and toasts the creek for its persistence, toasts the river rock for its endurance, the flies buzzing at his feet for god-knows-what. He tries to forget his day at work, his wife, his kids, but unlike the water under the bridge, his life constantly pools. Grows muddy, stagnant. "You can wait, bitch; you can all wait." He was going to turn around at the bridge but pulled over instead when the drink called. "You'd have a fit if you knew I kept this in the car, wouldn't you?" He takes another sip, slowly this time, swirls it in his mouth, savors the taste. "You don't know shit about me." The tumbler crashes against the bridge and falls in shattered pieces. The headlights of the Civic gaze at him like bulbous eyes, convicting him. He reaches into his pocket and pulls out a black balloon, squeezes it tight in his palm until the veins on his forearm bulge. Hesitating, he puts it back.

3

Poor Robert Shrub. A dozen broken drill bits stuck out from his legs by the time The Stranger with the white Robert mask got bored. By page three Charles had his hero passed out from the pain, and by the top of page four had him well again, still tied to the cross, but no longer a pin cushion; just a man tied to a cross waiting for his next lesson in morbidity. At first, Charles thought he'd make the entire scene with The Stranger part of a dream sequence, the mask some sort of reflection of Rob, but that was a horrible way to start any story. Dream sequences were copouts, like pulling the rug out from under the reader's feet. Readers hate that. Readers like to be in control. They like to think they know the way a story will unfold. Slush pile readers and editors especially. You're much better off running your manuscript pages across your ass after a wet shit than putting down on those same pages a dream sequence. Maybe Robert Shrub was crazy. Maybe he was reliving the torture over and over again as a way of righting himself. Maybe Robert Shrub was in Hell trying to work his way out.

Rachel wouldn't get it. She'd ask, "Why do you have him staple-gunned in the following section? Wasn't the drill enough? You have this guy in the mask drill a dozen holes into this poor sap and all you can come up with is torturing him further?" It was true. In the second chapter, Rob struggles on the horizontal makeshift crucifix. The man standing over him tilts his head slightly to the side, the white face staring down with the unemotional expression captured on the mask. Like Charles, Rob talks to himself. "Why do you have *my* face?" he says. "Why are you doing this to me? What is happening?" The man over him shakes his head, making a muffled ticking sound behind the mask. "You have my face," he says. "You are doing this to yourself; that is what is happening," and then he *ca'thunks* a half-inch staple into Robert's throat. Air wheezes through his O-shaped mouth as he takes in the shock and then the pain. He's about to scream when a second staple punctures the middle of his neck above the sternum. He takes another an inch lower, and another, and another; the last one buries into the soft flesh above his navel. Through watery eyes he discovers his zipper-like chest, as if he were a post-autopsy cadaver stapled together. Rachel definitely wouldn't get it.

Charles returned to the car, a little lightheaded but feeling high and full of life. He thought of turning around as he had initially planned. The empty road reminded him of *Akbar's Bridge*, a poem by Rudyard Kipling, the line ending with, "a bridge would save us all!" and so he crossed it and drove on.

"You can use a little more time," he said, unsure if he meant it for Rachel or for himself.

One hand on the wheel, he put the bottle of vodka in the glove compartment. The road ahead curved, but Charles kept the wheel straight, knowing the mixture of alcohol and drug was messing with him. A chipmunk ran across the road. He swerved to miss it and felt a small thump under the tires. The road ahead was clear. The rearview mirror revealed the same.

"Why in the hell would you choose to cross now, you stupid little bugger?"

Maybe the chipmunk wanted to die.

"Charles, lookout!"

It was Rachel, but she wasn't in the car.

He pulled hard on the steering wheel, the back tires screeching as they locked and spun the Civic around. The car came to an abrupt stop facing the opposite direction. He was the only car on the road. It was just Charles and the small smudge of red.

"A little late," he told Rachel. "Well," he said to his reflection in the rearview. "I guess now's a good a time as any to head back."

He sat there a moment, mostly to allow his nerves to settle, for trembling hands to still, for the road to straighten out. He pulled to the shoulder and left the car idle as he reached across the passenger seat to the glove compartment again. It wasn't the vodka calling this time, but the box of hypodermics. He fished the black balloon from his pocket with shaky fingers, bit the tip off a syringe, and plunged in the needle, pulled a small amount of clear liquid. No one was there to see, so he pumped his hand from flat to fist over and over again until the vein swelled. The needle slid in easily and the warm rush of elated pleasure was instant. It almost hurt to keep his eyes open, an orgasm working its way up his arm, to his heart, and from there, pumped throughout his body.

"Break the needle off in your arm," said The Stranger in the mask, but Charles knew he wasn't there. If he opened his eyes he knew he'd see the white face in the mirror. "Stab it in deep and break it off, Robert."

"I'm not Robert, you hack." He refused to open his eyes. Instead, he let the sensations ripple though his body. "I need to find you a name," he told his character.

"How about Charles?"

"Charles is *my* name."

He was met with silence, so he opened his eyes. It was all in his head. He was alone and laughed for even considering otherwise, but still the voices came to him.

"How about Robert?"

"I can't have *two* Roberts," he said to his reflection. "No one in their right state of mind would craft a story in which the only two characters were both named Robert."

"Then change the sap's name to Charles."

"Charles is *my* name," he said again. Like reasoning with a child. "What if I didn't name you at all? What if I decided to keep you as The Stranger? Do you want to be nameless the rest of your existence? On paper you are timeless, ageless, infinite. How would you like to live such an existence without a name at all? You could be The Walkin' Dude or The Man in Black or, in your case, The Man in the White Mask. I can make you anything I want."

"You're not the god of me."

"Wanna bet?"

"It's the other way around."

"I could erase you. I could burn every page with you on it."

"You would never do that, Charles, because I could always do the same to you and your paper world. I could choke you with pages. Wouldn't that make a great ending?"

"I could kill your character," said Charles. "You'd never touch another page. I could destroy your world."

In "Lucidity," Robert Shrub breaks free from his captor. It is a survival story, after all. The torture is in three parts: first the power drill, second the staple gun, and in a third and final blood-drenched scene, a hacksaw.

Waking this third time, Robert finds himself in similar fashion. Again he is tied to the mammoth cross, his wrists and ankles bound. He can only wait for what's to come, the man in the papier-mâché mask standing over him. "What do you want from me?" asks Robert. "What do you want, you sick fuck?" And it is then he realizes the white doctor's coat hanging over his captor's shoulders. "What is this place?" The room around him is completely white. The man standing over him only tilts his head, as if contemplating where to start. He starts with Rob's foot, grabbing him firmly a little above the ankle. As if bracing a piece of wood, he holds the leg still and slowly moves the rusty blade across the skin, cutting to the bone on his first pass. Robert screams. His back arches with the pain. The white doctor's coat, as well as the man's face, splatters red. The sick doctor's fingers bury into his skin to hold him in place. The blood on his face is a crooked smile dripping down a blank chin. "Settle down and hold still," he says and pulls the blade back. Blood arcs again on the second pass. The friction of metal cutting bone mixes with his cries. Quickly, the foot is gone, a solid sound as it hits the floor. A few of his teeth shatter as he grinds them together. Before he can cry out again, a patch of duct tape is placed over his mouth. His shaking foot pulsates, crimson squirting from the amputation.

Let me bleed out before I have to suffer that again. Let me—

Thick surgical tubing is wrapped around the hacked limb and a tourniquet is quickly produced to cut off the bleeding. And then his captor makes his first mistake as he moves in closer. After caressing his face with a bloody, glove-covered hand, he grabs Robert by his forearm. It doesn't take long for the hand to come off and he too hears it hit the floor. He lets him take it and watches the doctor as he puts a tourniquet on the nub, the nerve endings and tendons and veins crunching together at a point, all the while wondering in stupor how much blood he's lost, how much more he'd be capable of losing before his body let go of life. With the left side of his body completely free of constraints, Robert swings with his nub, hitting the mask and the face behind it. A jolt of pain shoots up the rest of his numbed arm, barely noticeable over the burst of adrenaline. He connects again and hammers the hacksaw free, connects again to the man's face, knocking it cockeyed, keeps swinging until the man falls to the floor. Robert uses his teeth to work the rope around his wrist, somehow unloosens it enough to slip free. With his one remaining hand he unties the last constraint and jumps down from the cross and lands on a single, unbalanced foot. Robert, already learning the necessity for symmetry, retrieves the hacksaw and topples over …

"What are you working on?" Rachel had asked.

The ending was right there waiting for him but she had ruined everything with those five simple words. What did she care? Rachel hated his work. She read his stuff, sure, but never liked any of it. "Lucidity" would be no different.

Charles knew how it would end and so he smiled as he pulled onto the road.

"I can't believe you'd do that to me, Charles."

"How do you know *your* fate? The story's not finished."

"I know because *you* know. You write my stories. And I write yours. It has an end."

4

Black film dappled with imperfection runs through the old drive-in projector. A bold line wavers down the center of the screen. All of this and the subtle flip-flip-flip of the reel tells him the movie is about to begin. His is the only car on the lot. Pulling a lever on his seat, he stretches his feet, reclines, takes off his belt to get more comfortable. He flips the radio to the proper channel and turns up the volume. Nothing is on yet but the static, so he takes a sip from his drink. At any moment countdown numbers will preamble the main feature. Maybe they'll show a short cartoon with dancing candy with arms and legs, popcorn tubs with smiling faces, a line of soda cups with bendy straws marching in line across the stage. The passenger seat to his right is empty. What he wouldn't give to be sitting next to Rachel back in high school, or her best friend, Jessica Hobbes, for that matter. He'd lean over, wrap an arm around her shoulder, nibble her ear a bit. If he was lucky he wouldn't get to watch the movie at all. He'd reach a hand up her blouse, maybe down the front of her skirt. Bases don't matter much when all you're trying to do is get the girl to do something to you in return. He reaches over to feel a breast. No one is there. Stars peck the boring sky as the noise of the projector gets louder, almost grating, the wavy line down the center of the screen becoming more prominent, the static on the radio more raucous. But he doesn't want to watch the movie. He doesn't want to see the end. He's seen it already. His hand moves along the seat, his fingers caressing the curves of the leather, searching for the teenage flesh he misses from high school. He's grown an erection, but the girl in the passenger seat isn't there, and there's no way he can get her to do what he wants her to do because she isn't there to see it. And then he feels a hand on his knee, feels it move up his thigh. Invisible fingers spider-crawling. One arm out the window, he slides his other between the seat cushion where his date should be, but she isn't there, and he doesn't feel what he wants to feel. His fingers slither into a sticky mess of snack crumbs and gum, perhaps left there by his children. The loud flip-flip-flip of the projector turns to tires running over reflectors in the center divider, the white line down the center of the screen just the dashed lines in the road passing under the Civic and across his windshield. The radio no longer plays static; it blares a horn.

5

It came right at him and within that instant of waking from his stupor he was able to slam his foot on the brake pedal and crank the wheel, but the minivan clipped the Civic. The driver's side window shattered, sending glass throughout the cabin. Charles watched in a slow motion as iridescent squares flew around him. Everything about the crash was instant: the lap belt holding him back from hitting the windshield, the sudden pain in his shoulder from the strap, his face making contact with the top of the steering column and bouncing as the airbag deployed and took the air from his lungs, the spin of the vehicle and the squelch of tires, their smoke wafting through the windowless frame as he spun and spun, his body pulling hard to one side and then to the other, the sudden sight of a sports utility vehicle—previously following him on the road but suddenly next to him—and the bumper smashing into his door, the pain in his legs as something cold and hard and heavy smashed into them, his head missing the Land Rover emblem but striking part of his own doorframe, a sharp whiplash as the larger vehicle flipped his Civic onto its side and finally upending it onto its roof, the seatbelt holding him in place with his arms hanging to the ceiling somehow.

There wasn't a warning from Rachel this time.

Upside-down, Charles could see that the off-white minivan had come to a stop off the side of the road. The front end of it was gone. It was an older model vehicle, so it didn't have airbags or safety glass. A body-sized hole remained in the windshield, from which the woman driver had been thrown; she lay in a crumpled heap on the asphalt twenty or so feet from where they'd made contact. A skid of red trailed her, a larger version of the chipmunk earlier. He could only see her back, but Charles guessed most of her face was gone by the angle of her body. A large dog was also in the minivan, but it was now a mass of smashed red wedged between the windshield and dashboard. A leg twitched and then stilled. The Land Rover was a different story. After smashing into the side of the Civic, it had crawled over his upturned car. Charles saw the underside of it through his passenger window. Its door opened and a man in shock walked casually to the side of the road to sit on the curb.

Charles' foot still pressed the brake. His other foot lay smashed against the accelerator, causing the engine to rev and the tires to spin against the body of the SUV. It made a horrible sound but he could barely hear it through the blood rushing to his head, and there was nothing he could do about it; his feet weren't working.

"Look out, Robert!" mocked a voice from the backseat. It was followed by a deep, haunting laugh.

The white-masked stranger from his story waited for him in the rearview. He was upright, which meant he was also strapped into the vehicle; his black hair stood straight, but he was otherwise composed. He shook his head and flicked his tongue against teeth hidden behind the mask. The face had a crack running down the middle of it. Blood seeped and ran upwards, like reverse tears.

He was about to tell the unnamed figment of his mind to stop calling him Robert, but instead Charles coughed blood.

"Poor Robert Shrub. What are we ever going to do? Look at us. We're a mess."

The man sitting upside-down on the curb was using his cell phone, hopefully calling an ambulance. There was yet another in the minivan, a young boy maybe ten or eleven.

"See what you did here?"

Go away.

"There's no going away. If I go away, you go away."

Then go away.

"All of this … the kid crying over his dog, over his

hamburger meat of a dog, his mother smeared across the road, the sap in his Land Rover calling his insurance agent instead of emergency, even you hanging here like a slab of meat ... that was me. I wrote this scene. Now all I need is an ending."

You're my *character.*

"And you're mine."

Then write me out of this and I'll give you an ending.

"I know the ending you'll create." Blood seeped through the mask, covering the expressionless face. It dripped rhythmically onto the ceiling.

It's not on paper. It's in my head. I can change it.

"I have an ending for you, Robert."

My name's Charles.

"You are who I make you."

A police siren droned in the distance, followed by that of an ambulance—two harmonies combining to create awful music. The afternoon sun filled the cabin with stifling heat. Something Rachel said once suddenly came back to him: What if heaven was in the sun, the source of all life? Charles tried the seatbelt, but his arms didn't want to cooperate, either. Everything about him was hot and numb, but he could at least feel the sweat beading and tickling his skin, and the constant rush of blood.

"No, you're not paralyzed; you're trapped," said The Stranger behind him. "Don't you find it unnerving to know there's nothing you can do? Don't you find it demoralizing that you can only sit here and wait? Your life, thrown into the trash. No end defined."

I hope I die.

"Welcome to my world."

Charles listened to the screaming sirens.

6

Out of the white and into the black. Life or death, it doesn't matter. Heaven or Hell, it doesn't matter. Nothing matters: not Rachel; not the kids; not his writing; not the light as it fades away or the black as it approaches. There is no meaning to any of it because he doesn't have an ending. He never wrote an ending. It's an unfinished story waiting at home at the bottom of the trash in his study. The white, it all turns to black, and within the darkness he awakes.

7

Where the fuck am I?

Charles sat upright in darkness, his fingers crawling like stubby caterpillars against the arms of a wooden chair. He wiggled bare toes against linoleum or tile flooring. Some sort of tape held him immobile, around his neck, waist, arms and legs. It covered his face and held together—in an uncomfortable mess—his nether regions. Patches of tape rubbed against various other places on his naked body, making him itch, pulling at hairs he never knew existed. The room was cold and carried the subtle breeze of air conditioning. The abrasive tape held one of his eyes open by an eyelash or two. The ability to close the lid would relieve most of the burning and allow trapped tears welling within to fall.

Charles tried to yell out. Only a muffled hum escaped the tape covering his mouth. He tried turning his head but the damned tape kept him from doing even that. He gave his legs a try. Rocking only produced squeaks, the chair either nailed or bolted to the floor. His arms ached. His face strained. His balls itched. The tape holding his feet to the floor pulled at his toes.

The sound of a light switch interrupted his efforts.

Blackness became hazy red.

Someone else was in the room, and had been during all his struggles, for there were no footsteps prior. Charles thought of screaming against the tape, but decided against it. He focused on the hazy red, attempted finding this person through one sore, open eye. His body trembled in the silence.

His vision darkened as the presence took a silent step forward. Warm, quiet breath met his nose and Charles let out a pathetic, muffled sound.

Sweat pooled at the tape around his waist, formed on his chest, back, everywhere. Beads fell from his forehead, gathered on his arms and legs. A stench of perspiration filled the room.

The darkness once again changed to hazy red.

Charles wondered a moment if it could be a dream. Maybe he was in bed next to Rachel. A combination of drugs and insomnia had been his devil these last few years; perhaps sleep, nightmare or not, had finally come for him. Maybe she was shaking him awake now. *Honey, you're having a nightmare*, as if she really cared at all, and once again he'd have to cry for a few winks of rest.

And then a length of tape was ripped away from his face. Unbelievable brightness took the room as horrendous pain took his face. Along with the tape came most of his eyebrows, his eyelid, and a majority of the soft skin connected to it. Blood poured hot down his face. A bitter-metallic taste teased his lips, leaking beneath the tape at his mouth. Immobile, Charles shook close to convulsion, his eye on fire.

Soon the room came into blurry focus: a small room no larger than most household bathrooms—no windows and no doors, he could see—but completely white, much like the patient rooms at New Bedlam Hospital off Johns. His son was born there. The walls, ceiling, polished tile floor—all glistened white. His captor's shadow loomed over him, like a specter, angled awkwardly from a light source behind them both.

A roll of duct tape lay on the floor. As he imagined, tape bound his arms, legs, waist, and feet to this enormous chair. He guessed the seat weighed hundreds of pounds, like a stripped-down electric chair—wooden, mammoth, and constructed for giants. Strips of tape covered a majority of his body, mimics of oddly placed bandages. He could not discern the condition of his crotch, for he was unable to peer low enough, but imagined himself wearing a Speedoesque pair of duct tape underwear. The wetness was either collected sweat or urine.

Without sound, his captor circled around Charles and appeared before him. Dressed in white, he was nearly camouflage to the rest of the room. This blurry man never came into focus as Charles dealt with the gore streaming down his own face, blinking away—with his remaining eyelid—the burning tears, and redirecting, with difficulty, blood from his mouth.

He's a doctor, Charles thought. *And he has no face.* It was either the blurred vision, or his captor was faceless.

He leaned in closer, gently pulled on the edge of the duct tape affixed to Charles' forearm, enough to imply his intentions.

Charles could only await the pain. It would hurt. Not as bad as the eye, but it would hurt. It would probably wake him up. But he'd rather sacrifice the pain for sleep. He'd have to take it. Charles gnashed his teeth.

The doctor let go and took a step back.

Charles shook like a scared child.

The doctor stepped forward, tilted his head a bit, and

nabbed the edge of another silver piece of tape on his thigh.

You're just a figment in my sleep-deprived, clusterfuck of a mind.

The doctor worked the edges of the tape more, testing for a reaction. And yanked.

Charles let out into the tape. For a moment, he forgot all about his pulsing face.

The doctor waited for Charles to calm before pulling another piece from his arm.

Again, Charles screamed and writhed against constraints. Sweat and tears became indistinguishable from one another. Fire burned at his thigh, at his forearm, at his exposed eye socket. The wounds throbbed synchronously to the rapid beating of his heart. "I'll put my fist through your fucking face when I get out of this!" he tried to say. Incoherency is all he managed through the tape.

It's my goddamn dream!

The doctor stepped back to watch, folding his arms almost reverently. When he next stepped forward, the faceless stranger violently ripped away the remaining strips of tape covering Charles Pierce's body—those along the backs of his toes, those on his sweaty cheeks, those on his chest, and finally those covering his crotch. Eventually he fell back into the blackness.

Sometime later—one eye closed, the other lidless, blinded by blood—Charles heard his captor affixing new straps of tape, covering him whole. Lastly, he heard the light switch.

8

I'm at home, napping at my desk, my body numb, slowly defrosting from sleep, drunk perhaps, hung-over perhaps, dreaming the horrible dreams of a sleep-deprived alcoholic falling off the wagon once again; maybe I actually did crash and I'm still in the car hanging upside-down, waiting for the ambulance to arrive; but why is everything black? Am I still dreaming?

Heat rose from his ankles to his calves, as if his feet were on hot coals. This same heat ran along his forearms and shoulders. Darkness surrounded him.

It was then he realized he was still in the chair.

As the numbness subsided, pain filled its place, along with awareness of immobility. Again, toes wiggled. Fingers crawled. The rest of his body stuck to the chair, but not by tape. There was no abrasive binding like before. He could move his head freely, but that was it.

I'm still naked ... The room, cold like before. The same room. The same damn chair. Maybe even the same faceless—

"My eyelid's back," Charles said aloud, merely because it was such an odd realization. His voice echoed, giving an approximation of the room size. The same white room, he guessed.

A jolt of immense pressure pushed at his shoulders and then to his knees. Charles clenched both fists, grasping at nothing. As he released pressure, his fingers curled upward at the ceiling, his hands like dying tarantulas. He could rotate his wrists, but doing so shot heat up his arms.

The smell of blood hovered in the room, as well as hints of pine-scented solvents.

Numbness started to wear off above his knees as each of his toes beat a pulse, as did his shoulders and wrists. Anxiety followed each attempt to move in the chair. His heart hammered. Everything Charles did to relax worsened the pain.

The black room swallowed him.

"What do you want with me?"

Silence.

He knew any second he'd pass out. It would be unbearable for any conscious mind. He'd pass out and forget it all. He'd wake up drunk on the couch or overdosed in the hospital.

The room spun, the pain excruciating, piercing, everywhere. Charles churned an amount of bile in his throat. His quadriplegic state caused stomach acid to waterfall down his chin.

The small room filled with blinding white light and slowly he was able to focus on the real horror.

Metal stakes were nailed through his wrists and into the arms of the chair. Charles thought of railroad ties as he waved to himself. Similar stakes were driven into the flesh above his knees, near the edge of his seat. Each shoulder housed the head of two more. Charles mouthed a short prayer, and was relieved not to find anything protruding from his genitalia. A set of 17-penny nails pinned each of his ten toes to the floor.

Next to his feet were two hammers: a sledge, and a claw.

Blood painted the room red. Even the ceiling contained sprays. Most of the gore pooled around the base of the chair.

Nothing but silence from the room.

9

The perfect martini. His third. Charles takes it down in a single tilt back with his head. It burns his throat like swallowing lava. A writer friend a while back taught him the recipe: pour vodka into a glass. Voilà. It burns away Rachel, their children, even his memories of Jessica Hobbes. Brenden's a small town, and there's only a handful like her to gawk at anyway … the next perfect martini removes it from his mind. Years ago it used to be his writing that kept him awake at night. Charles would find himself writing for hours on end, rubbing at his eyes to stay awake long enough to finish a chapter or two, words rambling through his mind faster than he could write sometimes. He'd turn off the lights and the ideas would pile like dirty laundry, and he'd have to get back up again and transfer the words from mind to paper to wind his imagination down enough for him to catch a few hours of sleep. Now a lack of writing keeps him up till two, sometimes three in the morning. Some nights he tries to force words on the paper. He gets a sentence, scratches it out, writes another, scratches it out, contemplates for an hour, writes a single word, scratches it out, and soon he's left with a page filled with black horizontal lines. It's like his mind is a blank sheet of paper sometimes and in order to sleep he must fill it, but he's too tired to think of words to saturate that page because he can't sleep—a recursive deprivation—and to actually sleep requires passing out, by drug or by drink. Insomnia got him writing in the day time, finally a chance to finish a story … the ending right there waiting for him.

10

His captor picked up the claw hammer from the floor after hesitating over the sledge.

Charles saw everything clearly, his eyes not watery like before, his vision unobstructed from the the duct tape.

The man before him wore white. Not a drop of Charles' blood was on him. A smooth white face—as white as the room around him—looked to the mess on the floor.

At first Charles suspected he didn't have a face, as if skin had been pulled taut where facial features should reside. Now, Charles found the face a shiny white. Smooth like glass. He watched as his captor looked to the blood, his face crimson—a reflective face, it seemed. The reflection changed to Charles on the chair.

Nail heads protruded from his toes, rail heads from his wrists, shoulders, and just above the knees. He was crucified to a chair. For a moment Charles thought of church as he last remembered it, but with a chairsufix hanging above the pulpit … a handicapped savior.

The claw end of the hammer swung through the air and buried into his knee. His leg tried to react, but the nails in his toes kept him in place, five holes tearing wider as the kneecap shattered.

Blood gushed onto his captor's mirrored face. He held the hammer by the handle and tried to pry it loose, but it was stuck.

Charles faded, the pain unlike anything he'd ever experienced. His body fought to stay awake, as if wanting to him to feel it all.

"Someone help me!"

The faceless stranger responded by kicking the claw hammer free. It landed across the room with chunks of shattered bone and torn flesh. Another red stripe painted the room. Torture danced through his leg to the beat of the blood pumping from the jagged hole in his knee.

His captor next stood over him with the sledge, his reflective face revealing the face of Charles staring at himself—a white, drained expression.

"Please stop! I'll pay you anything, give you anything you want. What do you want?" The last came out in childish sobs.

He just stood there, head tilted.

"I'll fucking kill you," Charles said, his voice cracking.

The sledge swung through the air, pounding the rail in his leg level with the bloody rags of skin around it. The head of the rail disappeared into his leg. His femur split down the center. Charles trembled, convulsed. What little of his body he could move he moved, tearing the gaps in his body wider.

His captor let go of the sledge, its fall breaking one of the few clean tiles at his feet. He grabbed Charles by the face and squeezed.

Charles attempted to look away.

Greedy hands pulled him back.

"Look at me."

Charles closed his eyes.

"Look at me."

Thumbs pressed into his eye sockets until they felt ready to pop. The Stranger nearly on top of him.

"Look at me!"

Charles gave in as blood and tears leaked from his eyes. A blurry, unfocused image of himself stared back. A scared man. He watched his reflection beg.

He could still feel the five toes split to ten on each foot, the rails in his shoulders worked somewhat free, the rails above his knees—the right still visible; the left buried into his flesh— working their constant pain, and now his eyes as they tried to focus on eyes trying to focus.

"Do you want free of this, Robert?"

"My names not—*you're The Stranger!* I created you. How can you do this? You're just one of my fucking characters. You're not real; you don't even have a name. You're not real … you're—"

"My name is Charles."

"No, you don't have a name; I haven't given you one. But that's not your face. You wear a white papier-mâché mask, not a mirror mask."

"But I am you and you are me and this is the face that you gave me. Do you want free of this?" One of his boots stepped onto his shredded toes.

His own reflected face smiled.

Charles sank a bit into the chair as severed nerve endings jolted his calves, thighs, all the way to his back.

"Fuck! Please, let me go."

His reflection remained stationary when his captor again tilted his head, as if contemplating.

"Let us do just that." It sounded demeaning, like something Charles would say.

The image of Charles shrank as The Stranger stepped back, and disappeared altogether as he retrieved the claw hammer from the floor. He returned shortly thereafter with it in his hands.

Charles, captured in the mirrored face, smiled wanly.

"I can give you whatever you want. You name it, it's yours. I'm your god, remember. I wrote you. I can give you life. I can make you anything you want to be. I can make your existence eternal."

A blood-soaked rag gagged him silent.

"All I want is to help you get out of this." He crouched low, examining the nails protruding from the toes on Charles' feet.

"This little piggy …" he said, swinging the hammer claw first. "Well, *this* little piggy didn't quite make it now, did he?"

Charles bit hard onto the rag and screamed a stifled scream as the nail was pried from the floor. He felt the nail pass through his big toe, the nerves reaching his neck.

"And *this* little piggy … kinda looks like roast beef."

It was a cheesy line, taken directly from "Lucidity" in a scene where Robert Shrub had his toenails stapled.

Barely conscious, Charles twitched as a second 17-penny nail was pulled from the next toe in line. The room faded, first at the edges of his vision and then working to the center.

Well, fuck all these other piggies.

Charles blacked out to the pinging of the remaining nails pounding flush against the floor.

11

Little black balloon. A magic portal. A transport away … to quieter places. Places without family, without friends, without worry. This little black balloon, Charles sticks the needle in, fills the syringe with a clear gelatinous substance. The tubing below his bicep helps expose the vein. Charles withdraws the syringe. He pumps his fist closed, open, closed, open, until a tiny mountain range of vein rises above a valley of skin. He sticks the needle deep, pushes the drug and feels it burn up his arm and into his chest. It burns down his legs, fills his head with hope. His heart beats faster as the drug transports him away from it all. To a dark place.

12

"I bet you're hungry." His captor said, holding out a plate of rare-prepared meat. The reflection revealed his sad face—the same exhausted-worried expression. "I bet your stomach is churning for nourishment."

He thought briefly of the burgers he and Rachel used to get at the restaurant next to the salon on Main Street. He couldn't think of the name, but remembered the burgers. His stomach growled.

"How long have I been here?"

His hands were no longer strapped by tape, no longer pierced by rails. He was free except for the rope binding him to the chair. No rails. No nails. No hamburger-meat-toes smashed to the floor.

Another sick dream?

Rope wound around his waist, tight around his sides. A scarlet towel covered his lower half—a formal napkin.

"Time isn't the issue here, Robert. Hungry?"

"My name is Charles."

His stomach let him know it was empty. He thirsted for the blood sweating from the dish held before him.

"How do I know this isn't a trick?"

The reflection on his face revealed Charles eyeing the meat.

"How do I know you haven't poisoned it, so you can watch me suffer as my bowels explode? How do I know—"

The mirrored face smiled. The reflection turned brownish-red as it glanced to the plate. Thin strips of what looked like slightly cooked steak sat in their juices.

Charles imagined the salty taste in his mouth.

The Stranger, still unnamed, took a step closer, offering.

Charles reached out, but the rope held him back; his fingertips met the edge of the plate.

The face was mad with rage.

"I'm messing with your mind," said The Stranger. He moved the plate closer.

Charles hesitated. It was tempting. It was also terrifying. But he needed the food. The thought of it dizzied him.

The face appeared undetermined.

"Do you think I'd hurt you, Robert? You are only hurting yourself. Here …" he said, and reached for a piece, tweezing a dripping strip between his fingertips. He brought it to the mirrored face—Charles' face.

Charles watched as it disappeared behind his own reflection. He watched his own mouth lick the man's fingers clean.

"Now, isn't that nice?"

His stomach eased, perhaps relieved. He eagerly reached for a piece. Ate it. Took another. Ate it. And another. Ate it.

The face smiled.

His stomach urged for more.

"Hungry?"

He was about to respond, but something wasn't settling. Pains grew in his abdomen, but it wasn't the meat. It wasn't his stomach. It was lower. Suddenly his thighs ached and then the pain migrated to his knees. A series of stings worked his legs as the room spun. Any moment Charles knew he would retch.

His captor fixed a strap of duct tape over his mouth.

Pain exploded from within. His thighs stung as if they were again pierced by rails, his knees as if they were again hacked by claw hammer. Everything below his knees was numb, as if his legs had been injected with Novocain. It was then Charles realized it wasn't a scarlet towel covering his lower half, but a *white* towel, soaked evenly though with his blood. Other white towels lay scattered at his feet, as well as used syringes.

13

Charles opened his eyes to a white room in Brenden Hospital. He knew that because there was a fold-up chair leaning against the wall that read: PROPERTY B.H.

Catheters stuck from the backs of his hands like nails, they were attached to hanging intravenous transfusions containing clear liquids. Gauze and medical tape patched his arms and chest. A white sheet covered the rest of his body. Farther up his arm was another catheter attached by tube to a hanging bag of blood.

There was a covered tray of food on his bedside table. Next to it was his manuscript for "Lucidity." Rachel must have dug it out of the trash and brought it. If he could find a pen he'd finally give it an ending.

Charles worked his hands free. The straps weren't tight.

A doctor in a white coat walked past the window to his room with Rachel at his side. His children were most likely waiting in the lounge. Seeing her with the doctor gave him chills.

Charles yanked the tubing from his arm and from the backs of his hands. He tore off bandages, opening unhealed wounds. When he lifted the sheet covering his legs, he found them missing; underneath were two nubs ending at his knees.

"What did you do to me?" he asked The Stranger, but he was alone in the room.

He thought of Robert Shrub and the torture he had put him through in his writing, leaving him on those last pages with one remaining hand and one remaining foot, those on his left side completely gone, sawed off and left in tourniquets. Half a man fighting his way to freedom. Robert had sacrificed one of his hands in order to break free, smashing it across the doctor's face to knock him to the floor, biting through the ropes binding his other hand, untying his bound leg and hopping off the cross, toppling over his captor as he reached for the hacksaw …

Charles brought his hands to his face, glad he still had them. He was now half a man, like his character. His ability to write was not taken from him, at least, and he knew deep down why he had lost his legs instead of his hands.

He had to finish "Lucidity," so said his captor.

It was on the bedside table. A brown stain streaked the cover page like drippings from the meat of his legs he was scammed into eating.

Does he write my life? Is he writing it now?

The pages were stapled together, the corner bent. Rachel must have read it. Her reading it didn't bother him; the staple did.

"You *never* staple manuscripts," he told the empty room.

The EKG next to him beeped.

Charles reached for "Lucidity," but the bedside table was a cart on wheels and he pushed it back a bit with his fingertips.

Twisting his body somewhat off the bed, he managed to grab the edge of the manuscript, but the cart rolled even farther and he fell off the bed and onto the floor, the cart crashing in an awful cacophony of falling metal. The tubes connecting to the catheters ripped free and dripped over him. The bags of blood and the silver skeletal arm holding it fell against the bed.

Charles held onto the manuscript the entire trip. The food tray had spilled over it, splashing mashed potatoes and strips of meat in red juices that soaked into its pages. Charles forced down the bile climbing his throat as he was reminded of his missing legs, which were now ghost limbs that somehow throbbed with pain.

The EKG announced to the room that he was dead by releasing a high-pitched, monotonous tone, his pulse a horizontal line.

He laughed as Rachel and the man in the white doctor's coat rushed into the room.

"Honey, are you okay? What happened?"

"I fell off the wagon," he said casually. He held "Lucidity" for her to see. "Did you like it?"

"Let's get you back onto the bed," said the doctor.

Charles expected a mirrored or white papier-mâché mask with his own facial features.

"Did you like it?" he asked her again.

"The ending was strange. You kind of left it as a cliffhanger."

"It didn't have an ending. I haven't written it yet."

"Forget the damn story. You've been out for three days. The accident … I'm so sorry, honey."

"Accident?"

"We can talk about it later. Here, let's get you off the floor."

She and the doctor each grabbed an arm, hoisting him onto the hospital bed.

He couldn't have weighed much with both legs gone.

Once situated, the doctor reaffixed the various medicines to their appropriate catheters and called a nurse to prepare another bag of blood for the one that had fallen over. After the monitoring cable was reconnected to his index finger, the EKG resumed its beeping, reassuring Charles that he was alive. His pulse rapid.

The doctor applied new bandages and checked those around his amputated limbs.

"As you can see, Robert, we had to take your legs."

"*What?*"

"The impact from the accident pinched your legs and we had to amputate in order to save you. I'm sorry. We're just glad to see you alive." He gave a crooked smile that looked much too like the blood smile on the papier-mâché mask.

"What did you call me?"

"I'm sorry?" the doctor asked.

"Robert, everything's going to be okay," Rachel said.

"What the fuck is wrong with you people?"

The doctor glanced at the chart.

"Robert Shrub, right?"

"My name is Charles. Charles Pierce. Rachel, what's going on?"

"Honey, Charles Pierce is your doctor."

He read the name badge: DR. CHARLES PIERCE, MD.

"This is the wrong ending. I don't know what's happening, but this isn't the right ending. I'm dreaming. This is some sort of lucid dream. I'm still hanging upside-down in the car. It's not supposed to end this way. I know the ending, I just haven't written it yet. None of you would know."

"I think you need some rest," the doctor said. "You've been in a coma for three days. Hysteria is typical, given the circumstances."

"Can I borrow your pen?" Charles asked.

"Honey, maybe he's right. Maybe you should rest."

"Maybe you should get the fuck away from me. You're the reason I'm in the hospital." He held up the manuscript and slapped her across the face with it. "You kept me from finishing this story, remember?"

Rachel cried into her hands and ran out of the room.

"Sir, you need to settle down," the doctor said. "Nurse!"

"Let me borrow your pen a moment," Charles said, taking it from the doctor's shirt pocket. "I need to write the ending before I wake up from this."

"I think you better—"

Charles grabbed the doctor by the collar and stabbed the pen into his neck. It went halfway in and stopped. He held the man's throat and pulled him closer.

"I know who you are," Charles said, inches from his face. "Look at me."

Gasping, the doctor closed his eyes.

"Look at me."

Charles pressed his thumbs into the man's eye sockets. They pressed deep into his head. The Stranger nearly on top of him.

"Look at me!"

He gave in as blood leaked from his eyes. What stared back was a blurry, unfocused image. Charles reached for the manuscript at his side.

The doctor fell to his knees, taking Charles with him to the floor. They fell hard, but Charles straddled him with his shortened appendages. The Stranger no longer fought; he lay still with all the features in his face now gone—a featureless mask—and the pen protruding from his neck.

Charles ripped out the last page of "Lucidity" and crumpled it within his hand, opened The Stranger's crooked smile and stuffed it in as far as he could.

Finally finished with his story, Charles waited for Rachel to return so she could see the ending. She wouldn't like it.

THE START OF FOREVER

or

THE SEED, PART TWO

You started out as a seed

In a round about way you were simple
Small, imperfect, alone
Blown around with early spring
Young, agile
The red robin carried you on its wing
Dropped

Fallen to the earth, your new home
Cold, damp, dark
Nature's beasts trampled you down
Planted, buried
You shivered, seared and lonesome
Forgotten

Rained down upon by the water gods
Pounded, beaten, drowned
You struggled and fought and failed
Left, abandoned
You stopped fighting and gave in
Died

You started out as a seed

AFTERWORD

BUT NOT QUITE THE END

Disturbed? I hope you are feeling disturbed or a little uneasy after reading such a rancid collection of... oh, you were referring to me. Yeah, I am various shades of sick. I probably need a therapist. But that's okay; most of my fiction is psychological horror, so the relationship I share with my literary self doesn't have to be healthy. Sure, there are voices in my head, but I let them rattle out and onto pages every once in a while. If I didn't, I would really be in trouble. Sometimes I look into the mirror and expect the glass to shatter. There is someone on the other side and he's tired of looking at his sad reflection: me. He wants to bash his way through and wrap his fingers around my throat to stop the voices rattling around in his own head... maybe he's the one in need of a therapist.

It doesn't matter. You found your way to the back of the book, which means you waded through the mud and survived my poetry and fiction, or you just flipped to the end to see if I left an e-mail address (written@nettirw.com) you could use to express your dire hatred of this book. Either way, here you are. I own your eyes. I have the opportunity to reflect on my writing and to answer the questions people ask me most often: Where do you get your ideas? Why do you write? What the hell is wrong with you?

I often leave things open-ended in my writing. I like to put the reader in compromising and/or uncomfortable situations, and then have them question the reality, which is a funny thing since I write fiction. It's all imaginary; there is no reality. If my fiction has pulled you out of your world long enough to forget this fact, for even the briefest of moments, then you know the answer to those complex questions. There are things on the other side of the glass that want out. Test how long you can stare at yourself in the mirror with the lights turned off. Pay close attention to the eyes. You are not alone. Existence is a puddle with a shimmering hand reaching through the surface. Sometimes you grab the hand; sometimes it grabs you. The ideas that drip out of my head usually come from holes in the nonlinear; they're everywhere. I write for those in the puddle, for those stuck behind the mirror. There are a lot of things wrong with me.

Why do I write such dark fiction? To be honest, the world is a very dark place and I write about that which scares me: subsistence, the human condition, the extreme fragility of our minds. We're all a little dark with the lights off. I happen to enjoy my darkness more than others, the voices in my head boisterous and unforgiving. The stories and poems in this collection are reflections and intimations of my disturbed mind, thrown into a wood chipper and splattered onto the pages for your enjoyment. It's easy for me to write.

Admitting that is scary in itself. It supports the theory that I am in desperate need of therapy. But enough about me. There are a lot of people that support my insanity. A special thanks is in order to the various authors, editors and fellow participants of the Borderlands Press boot camps in Maryland: Tom

F. Monteleone, you are one crazy bastard and you have helped me realize over these last few years that writing is a disease; F. Paul Wilson, your advice is always a brilliant mix of cruel and sincere; Douglas E. Winter, your editing pen cuts like a knife and because of you I forever bleed on the pages; David Morrell, you may have introduced the world to Rambo, but your words are a mastery of elegance (sorry about all these semicolons. I know you hate them); Gary Braunbeck, you have taught me to find emotion in my writing and I cannot thank you enough… you are a literary god; Mort Castle, you are a strange one; Elizabeth Massie, you are sickly sweet; John Douglas, you are the first New York editor I have ever met who actually appreciated my work and complimented my style; Ginger Buchanan, you were the first New York editor to put me in my place; and to all the grunts … it has been a wild, cold, sleep-deprived ride. And lastly, I have to thank those close to me (you know who you are). You are the disturbed ones. You help shape my life and put up with me at my worst, which in turn translates to the page. If you haven't read the authors I name-dropped, then now is your chance. These are the true masters of the craft. I'm merely an apprentice.

So, now you realize my mental state is somewhat chaotic. Turn off the lights and stare at yourself in the mirror for a while. Try not to imagine a naked man with a plunger standing next to you, or a faceless woman oozing sludge from a hole in her forehead. Don't think about claw hammers burying into kneecaps, or television sets flying out windows, or stuffed bears smiling through crisscrosses of thread. Don't think about any of those things.

This is the second edition of *Scales and Petals*, so as a bonus I've included both the original script and graphic adaptation of

the first story in this collection, "Plasty." I collaborated with
L.A. Spooner to bring this twisted story to life in a new kind
of way. Enjoy! But before that are three previously unpublished
flash fiction pieces, two of which were early excercises at the
Borderlands Press boot camps.

PORTRAYAL

or

BAD MEAT KARMA

[a companion piece to "Empty Canvas"]

"Try not to smile," he says. "Relax and remain still. You can breathe and blink and whatnot, but don't move. I want the real you."

The real me wants to get up from this chair. The real me wants to make him choke on those brushes. The real me wants to pour the paint down his throat.

My sister's the painter, not this guy.

"You're smiling again," he says. "People don't go around smiling all the time. I want to paint Gioconda Padovan the way the world sees her, not how she sees herself."

"Seriously?" I say.

My demise is that most adverbs said aloud transform mouths into crescents.

"When we're done with this," he says, "you will be smiling from ear to ear."

I'll make him smile from ear to ear, with pruning shears. And after he's done with this stupid portrait, I'll adverb the *fuck* out of him. Smile from ear to ear … Who says that shit?

Those words want to leave my mouth, but my mouth traps them inside because I'm posing a lack of emotion.

Who paints portraits?

He whipped out the brush. I thought it was a ploy to convince me into removing my clothes to pose for something "artistic." I'd rather let him take a digital picture of me naked and hide it somewhere on his computer. I'd pose for that. I'd ask for a copy through email and then forward it to my sister so she'd see his address.

My sister's been laid more times than plywood because of digital pictures. Pockmarks and stretch marks don't matter much when they're airbrushed out of existence and sent to some douchebag on the internet. That's how she met this guy. I know he's seen her naked because her bed kept smacking against my bedroom wall last night. She moans like a mule hit in the head with a brick too many times.

This quote/unquote artist with brushstrokes as thick as his eyebrows, he looks over his shoulder every so often as he paints me.

I wouldn't have slept with him. His feet are small.

That's some *bad meat karma* right there.

"Bad meat" is my sister's term for a bad lay.

She fucks him and I get stuck playing host the morning after because we share an apartment. She leaves for work. He stays. Thanks again, Sis.

"Let me paint you," he had said.

That's all it took. What can I say? I'm a Padovan.

I sit in the chair, hands in my lap, legs crossed, hair dangling over my shoulders.

I am not smiling.

He squirts acrylic on the pallet, splotches white on my canvas face, and I can't help but wonder if Picasso ever painted cum. They're supposed to be eyes, but his artistry borderlines the talent of a child grinding crayons against construction paper.

After an hour of biting the insides of my cheeks to keep from laughing at his constant, concentrative, mid-coitus expression, my painted face is nothing more than flesh-tone matte with a hotdog mouth, brown mop hair and ejaculate eyes.

When he next turns around to show me his progress, I'm not wearing any clothes.

"Try not to smile," I say.

The woman on the canvas is hideous.

[for my fellow grunts: Meghan Arcuri and R.B. Payne]

YELLOW

[from an abandoned anthology]

Coworkers nicknamed me DY, or Double-Yellow. They think
I'm Asian *and* scared. There are so many things wrong with
that. The Human Resources department is dealing with a polit-
ical correctness nightmare, but they're working on it, they say.
There's not much time.

> *What is time, but agony*
> *What is Agony, but passion*
> *Passion, is that not the same as love?*

I'm technically half-Japanese, born and raised in downtown
Baltimore, but most of my peers see the eyes and think rice.
One time I brought takeout for lunch and one of the accoun-
tants, said, "So, do you just call that food?" I fake-smiled and
fake-laughed and informed him it was *Chinese* food, not *Japanese*
food, and that I ate it with a fork. The joke was crude.

> *Crude, a nice way of saying nasty*
> *Nasty, a nicer word for ugly*
> *Ugly, is that not beauty from the other side?*

That explains the first yellow. The second comes from a traumatic experience. Jumpy, sure. Sometimes coworkers pound the cubicle glass to get my attention. Think it's a riot when I startle. The sound of knuckles against glass reminds me of the night I watched my mother die. Every time they hit the glass, I think my life is going to shatter.

What is anxiety?
Is it apprehension?
Is it angst?

I was thirteen and we were eating frozen yogurt at a place where you could add your own toppings. We sat at a white rot-iron two-person table next to one of the large pane windows to watch for my dad, who was supposed to meet us there. We waited long enough, and decided to have ours without him. Any number of things could have prevented her death: me taking an extra second to drizzle more chocolate, mom scooping more mochi, us choosing any of the other three tables, the posture she held in her chair, or if I sat in her chair … the slightest of incidents. Dad could have shown.

Death begins when life ends
A wall at one end, a wall at the other
Life, does it not also begin with death?

The bullet shattered the glass, which sprinkled around us like toppings. She didn't know she was shot, at first, concerned only with me as she lunged over the table and tackled me to the floor. Strawberry syrup spilling around us.

Blood as a liquid, warm, viscous
Pumping through the body, out the body
Blood, at the end, thickens, solidifies.

That's how she died; a stray bullet from a drive-by shooting. And every time a coworker pounds on that glass, it brings me back to that moment. Call me scared. Call me yellow. I'll show you a color we all have in common.

SMALL PRINT

or

PYLON / THE LONELIEST PYLON
[for Thomas F. Monteleone]

So this man in an ugly fuckin' business suit comes walkin' to my cubicle all smug and says to me, "You Tom Wilson?" and I says to him, "Yeah, I'm Tom Wilson, what's it to ya? Who let you in?"

Mr. Suit drops an orange traffic cone by my feet. It's one of them tire-trampled ones, what you'd expect to see tipped in a gutter.

"What the fuck is this?"

"A pylon," he says, as if that makes any sense.

A black-gloved hand pulls out a Glock. And then I remember the date: twenty-seventh of January, what would be me and my wife's tenth anniversary. I'd picked that date back when I thought the world was done with me.

"You know why I'm here."

My expression must have told 'em.

Think I do, but I called it off last month."

"There's no calling it off," he says. "Ever think to read the fine print?"

What fine print? There wasn't no fine print. What's with the fuckin' pylon?

Mr. Suit sighs, digs in his pocket, slaps the contract I signed against the partition glass.

"Read," he says, aimin' at my face.

I lean forward, but the print's too fuckin' small. No one can read that shit. No one ever reads that shit.

This guy, he lets me know with the gun he's not buyin' it. He knows I won't read the small print 'cause he knows he's right. Prob'ly says there's no way out. Contract's signed in blood and he's gonna kill me.

"But I changed my mind," I tells him. "Called your number, left you messages."

"There's no changing minds in my profession. I get paid to finish jobs," Mr. Suit says, and boots the cone in my direction. "Now wear it, like a dunce cap."

This goddamn pylon, it's big enough to cover my head and slump over a shoulder. I can smell the gutter.

"No fuckin' way. You want money? I'll get you more."

A round shatters the computer monitor behind me.

"Wear it on your head. I won't ask again."

"Is this some kinda joke?" I says, but this guy ain't jokin'. "At least tell me why I gotta wear it."

"Frankly, Mr. Wilson," he says. "I don't want to see your bloody face after I put a bullet through it. And, if you must know, I forgot to bring a blindfold and found this on the way here."

"I don't get it."

Another sigh.

"The cone goes over your dome. The barrel goes through the hole. A bullet goes through your skull. You die … as originally contracted. I go home, have dinner with my family. Everyone's happy."

Not everyone.

The giant road sombrero drips with urine and smells like shit. Mud and street juice is all it is, but the imagination works wonders with a gun pointed at—

"I didn't pay to go out this way."

"No, you didn't. You paid me to kill you. Small print on that contract you failed to read says I'm at liberty to choose my method. The only stipulation is that you die."

"What if I say no? Watcha gonna do, kill me?"

The second round blasts through the top of my foot and I crumple.

"Gah!"

"Here's what happens if you say no. I keep putting bullets in you until you wear the pylon. I brought a few clips, so this can get fun, but I'd rather be home having dinner. Nod if you understand."

Death is better than sufferin' so I lift the thing over my head, hair slicking to the gunk, hobo pee runnin' along my neck, pancakes of brown slidin' down.

"Make it fast," I says.

He kicks the pylon, breakin' my nose, and now I'm smellin' coppery shit.

The pylon's big inside. I tilt my head to the circle of light. Peekin' through is Mr. Suit's mug, then the phallic tip of the Glock like I'm at the receiving end of a glory hole.

The barrel wiggles.

"I'm messing with you," this guy says. "There's nothing in the fine print that says you can't call it off. But, it does say I can mess with you if you cancel."

PLASTY SCRIPT

PAGE ONE

PANEL 1:

Full-page: Over THOMAS PARK-ER's shoulder, a pale girl stands slouched behind the counter of a coffee shop: streaks bleeding through dark hair, black mascara, eyeshadow, dark lips, a silver hoop in her eyebrow, more in her lobes and inner ear, a stud in her nose, THE LINE BEGINS TO BLUR printed on a T-shirt that exposes her pierced navel and silver chain waistlet. She looks annoyed.

CAPTION:

PLASTY

SUB-CAPTION:

WRITTEN BY MICHAEL BAILEY

SUB-CAPTION:

ILLUSTRATED BY L.A. SPOONER

PAGE TWO

PANEL 1:   Close-up of a pens stabbing a mug full of coffee beans on a dirty counter.

PARKER: Off-scene: "What's on your face?"

PANEL 2:   Close-up of the BARISTA GIRL's face and the set of dotted lines drawn onto her cheekbones, in the shapes of upside-down triangles below each baggy eye, clown-like.

BARISTA GIRL: "What do you mean?"

PARKER: Off-scene: "Never mind. Sorry."

PANEL 3:   The BARISTA GIRL grabs his elbow, pivoting him back around to face her.

PANEL 4:   Her annoyance has transformed to nervousness as she stands straighter, worried, one eyebrow cocked. She rotates a hoop in her ear with one hand, the other feel ing her cheekbone.

BARISTA GIRL: "Is there something on my face?"

PARKER:	"Dotted lines."
PARKER:	"Triangles"
BARISTA GIRL:	"What?"
PANEL 5:	Close-up of PARKER's hand. He gently traces the triangle-shaped surgeon's marks with the tips of his fingers, her cheeks blushing.
PARKER:	"Here."
UNKNOWN:	Off-scene: "Café mocha!"

PAGE THREE

PANEL 1:	As he exits the café, THOMAS PARKER bumps shoulders with a woman running blindly down the sidewalk to chase her son.
PANEL 2:	The BLONDE WOMAN catches her boy by his shoulder, spinning him around (similar to PANEL 4 PAGE ONE), and spills some of PARKER's mocha over the lid and onto PARKER's hand.
PANEL 3:	The BLONDE WOMAN's nose is

covered with a patch of gauze and horizontal strips of tape to keep it in place. The rest of her face is flawless, strikingly beautiful.

BLONDE WOMAN: "I'm so sorry."

PANEL 4: Close-up of the sidewalk, with heavy drops of blood splattering the ground and PARKER's shoes, like raindrops, some still in freefall.

PANEL 5: Close-up of the BLONDE WOMAN's nose, and the gauze there quickly absorbing her nose bleed.

PARKER: "You're—"

PANEL 6: The woman's nose drips freely as she puts a hand on her son's shoulder, oblivious to her condition.

BLONDE WOMAN: "I know. Bobby's always taking off like that."

PARKER: "Your nose."

BLONDE WOMAN: "What about it?"

SOUND EFFECT: Drip, drip-drip … drip

PARKER: "Uh … you have a nosebleed."

PANEL 7:   The BLONDE WOMAN rubs her nose, pulls a set of sticky red fingers back to inspect them; confused, she's unaware of anything out of the ordinary, her blouse heavily striped with red.

BLONDE WOMAN: "What are you talking about?"

PARKER: "Your nose."

PARKER: "You should see your doctor."

BLONDE WOMAN: "What doctor?

PANEL 8:   Their backs to him, she and her son walk down the sidewalk, leaving a trail of red dots in their wake. Her son's shoulder is smeared with a bloody handprint as he looks to the clouds to find imaginary shapes, while she hails for a cab with a bloody hand.

PARKER: From afar: "Ma'am—"

PAGE FOUR

PANEL 1:   Full-page of THOMAS PARKER.
                        He kneels to the bloody mess
                        at his feet, raising three bloody
                        fingers to his face, pondering the
                        trail of red leading to the woman
                        and her son in the distance,
                        wondering if what he saw was
                        real, or perhaps imaginary, like
                        finding shapes within clouds.
                        There are finger smears in the
                        blood beneath him, his own. The
                        café to his back is full of life.

BLONDE WOMAN: Over her shoulder: "Come on,
                        Bobby. We only have an hour
                        before cello."

PAGE FIVE

PANEL 1:   The back of THOMAS PARKER.
                        He looks up to massive grey thun-
                        derclouds challenging an other-
                        wise clear sky. POV: looking
                        through glass from within the café
                        as he reaches for the doorknob.

PANEL 2:   A nearly empty counter of
                        coffee condiments, sugars and stir

sticks scattered around a spilled drink. In one corner are PARKER's bloody fingertips searching for something clean.

PANEL 3: Everyone in the café looks at him as if he's crazy and causing a ruckus as he walks back to the front counter.

PANEL 4: The undead-looking girl, who had taken his coffee order earlier, turns away from him to call out an order.

BARISTA GIRL: "Something-something double-shot macchiato or something."

PARKER: Approaching the counter: "Ma'am?"

PANEL 5: Close-up of the BARISTA GIRL, no longer with bags under her eyes. Skin within the previously dotted lines on her face is gone; in place are two upside-down triangles of raw, skinless red, as if someone's cut away the flesh and peeled it away. Dark red tears leak from the wounds, zigzagging down the curves of her young face.

BARISTA GIRL: Agitated: "What."

PANEL 6:   Zoomed out (perhaps her face
                       out of focus behind his hand),
                       PARKER points at her joker eyes,
                       filling most of the cell.

PARKER: Off-scene: [a silent scream caught
                       in his throat]

PANEL 7:   Half his body blurred as he turns
                       away in fright. His un-blurred
                       half absentmindedly slaps a lady
                       in the chest, which has a large
                       lump tumbling downward from
                       beneath her blouse.

PANEL 8:   A bloody silicone implant slaps/
                       plops flat against the floor at his
                       feet. He's not really sure what it is
                       until ...

SOUND EFFECT: Flap!

PAGE SIX

PANEL 1:   Half-page: PARKER's shaky
                       outstretched hand holds the slimy
                       implant out to the woman who
                       lost it (and her husband next to

her), the implant slipping from his hand as he's realizing what he's holding, his face horrorstricken.

PANEL 2:   The implant drops again to the floor.

SOUND EFFECT: Flop.

PANEL 3:   Sticky-webbed fingers wipe across jeans.

IMPLANT WOMAN: Off-scene: "Watch where you're going."

PANEL 4:   PARKER stares at the woman's chest, which is now flat on one side and flowering with blood.

PAGE SEVEN

PANEL 1:   The café crowd stirs.

PANEL 2:   PARKER holds out an empty (yet messy) cup of hands to the couple, nearly touching her remaining breast.

PARKER: "Your wife's breast—"

PANEL 3:   The ANGRY HUSBAND slaps away PARKER's hand

SOUND EFFECT: Slap!

ANGRY HUSBAND: "Get away from my wife."

PANEL 4:   PARKER is pushed against the front counter, spilling the coffee beans in the mug holding pens.

PANEL 5:   The bloody implant lands on someone's poppy seed muffin, the owner of the muffin unaware and pinching off a bite.

BARISTA GIRL: From afar, off-scene: "Take this outside, you guys."

PANEL 6:   A hyperventilating look on PARKER's face as he sprays the room (and the page) with an explosion of words between breaths, hands at his side.

PARKER: "I'm sorry."

PARKER: "I don't know what's happening to me."

PARKER: "I don't know …"

PARKER: "I don't know ..."

PARKER: "What's happening?"

PARKER: "I, I—"

PAGE EIGHT

PANEL 1:   Quarter-page: A woman with a
                   burnt face stares at him from
                   across the café: from a chemical
                   peel, she bleeds from exposed
                   pores as if a mask of a face had
                   been ripped away ...

CAPTION: CHEMICAL PEEL

PANEL 2:   Quarter-page: Flashback of the
                   BLONDE WOMAN outside with
                   the nosebleed ...

CAPTION: RHINOPLASTY

PANEL 3:   Quarter-page: Flashback of the
                   woman with the single breast and
                   her shirt stained red ...

CAPTION: MAMMOPLASTY

PANEL 4:   Quarter-page: A woman sits

upright in a chair with puffy, overly-swollen lips …

CAPTION: LIP AUGMENTATION

CENTER PANEL: Perhaps PARKER trapped in a diamond/center panel, with each of these four quarter-page panels bearing down on him in the middle.

PAGE NINE

PANEL 1: Quarter-page: A man sits on a couch in the café, with red gauze taped loosely on his chin (which has slid down his neck), exposing his mental protuberance (chin bone) …

CAPTION: CHIN AUGMENTATION

PARKER: "I—"

PARKER: "Those people on the couch."

PANEL 2: Quarter-page: Sitting next to the guy with the chin augmentation is a woman in a white pair of pants with a red stain at her crotch.

CAPTION: LABIAPLASTY

PANEL 3:   Half-page (bottom): The BARISTA
                        GIRL with THE LINE BEGINS TO
                        BLUR T-shirt leans over the
                        counter to peer down at PARKER
                        who has crumpled to the floor,
                        grabbing his stomach. Her eyes
                        are hidden by her position. Others
                        from the café crowd around, and
                        we only see their backs as he pulls
                        at his shirt.

PARKER: "Euuuuuggh!"

BARISTA GIRL: "Should I call an ambulance?"

PAGE TEN

PANEL 1:   Full-page: THOMAS PARKER is flat
                        on his back. He holds his hands
                        out to his sides, and they are tacky
                        and covered in a gelatinous fatty
                        substance. His shirt is pulled up to
                        reveal his stomach, which is
                        covered in purple-brown bruising
                        over most of his abdomen, his
                        belly button just a loose flap of
                        dead skin over a blackened hole.

Those in the café crowd around,
their faces normal, their bodies
normal, and their expressions
horrified as they circle and stare
over him. In the distance the
BARISTA GIRL, with the piercings
and the mascara   and the streaks
in her hair, looks at THOMAS
PARKER with a phone pressed to
her ear. Her eyes are beautiful.

CAPTION: LIPOSUCTION

PLASTY

WRITTEN BY MICHAEL BAILEY
ILLUSTRATED BY L.A. SPOONER

WHAT'S THAT ON OUR FACE?
NEVER MIND. SORRY.
IS THERE SOMETHING ON MY FACE?
DOTTED LINES.
TRIANGLES.
WHAT?
CAFÉ MOCHA!
HERE...

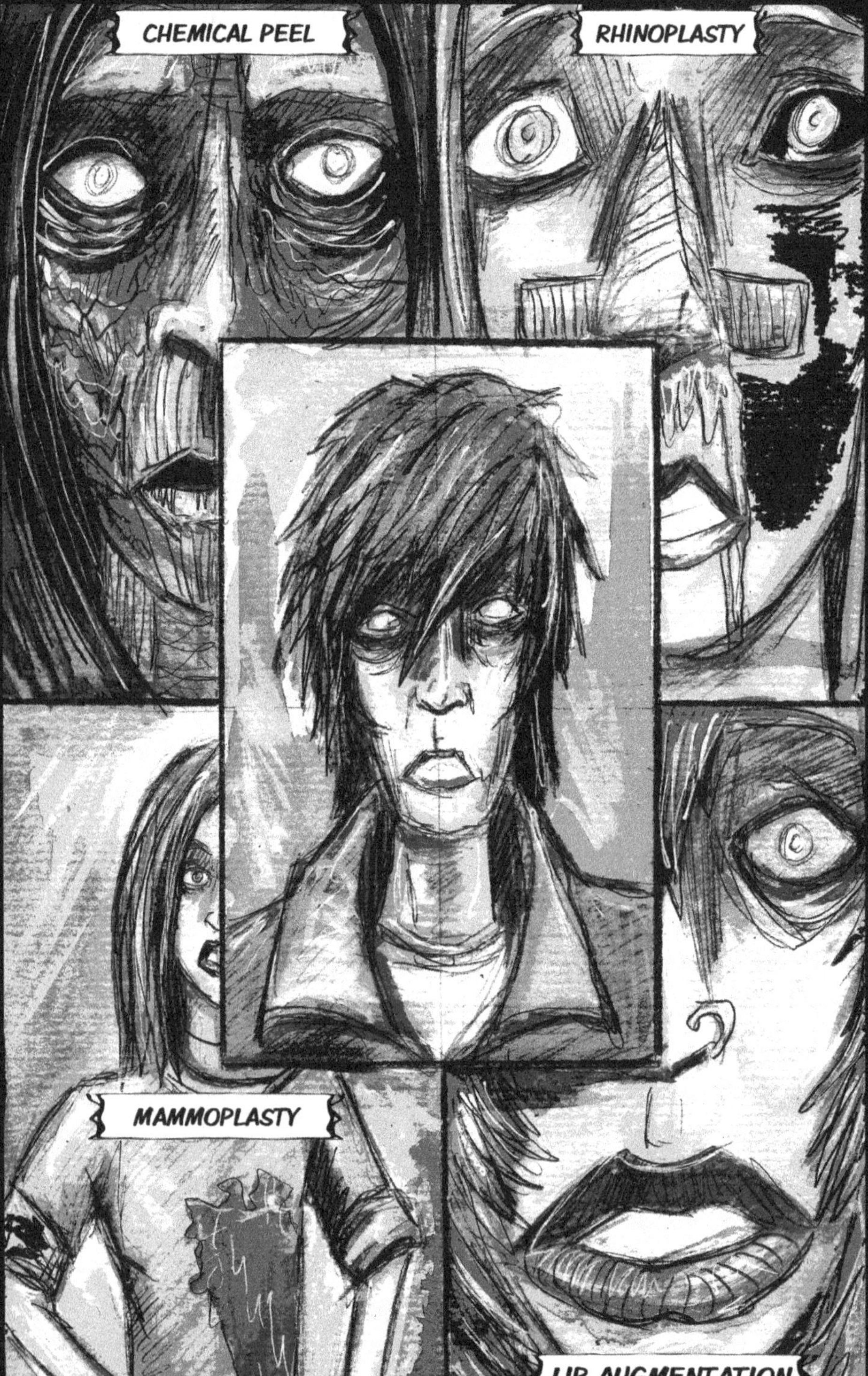
CHEMICAL PEEL
RHINOPLASTY
MAMMOPLASTY
LIP AUGMENTATION

CHIN AUGMENTATION
LABIAPLASTY
I- THOSE PEOPLE ON THE COUCH...
EUUUUUGGH!
SHOULD I CALL AN AMBULANCE?

LIPOSUCTION

ABOUT THE AUTHOR

Michael Bailey is a multi-award-winning author, editor and publisher, and the recipient of over two dozen literary accolades, including the Bram Stoker Award, Benjamin Franklin Award, Eric Hoffer Book Award, Independent Publisher Book Award, the Indie Book Award, the International Book Award, and others. His novels include *Palindrome Hannah*, *Phoenix Rose* and *Psychotropic Dragon*, and he has published two short story and poetry collections, *Scales and Petals*, and *Inkblots and Blood Spots* (illustrated by Daniele Serra, with an introduction by Douglas E. Winter).

He is also the founder of the small press Written Backwards, where he has created psychological horror anthologies such as *Pellucid Lunacy*, *The Library of the Dead*, four volumes of *Chiral Mad* (the fourth co-edited by Lucy A. Snyder), and a few dark science fiction anthologies such as *Qualia Nous* and *You, Human*. He also served as the co-editor of both *Adam's Ladder* and *Prisms* (with Darren Speegle). Most recent publications include *Oversight*, a collection of novelettes including *Darkroom* and *SAD Face*, and the standalone novelette *Our Children, Our Teachers*. He lives in forever-burning California.

You can follow him on social media at twitter.com/nettirw, facebook.com/nettirw, or online at www.nettirw.com.